Shakespeare on the Double!™

Romeo and Juliet

Shakespeare on the Double!™

Romeo and Juliet

translated by

Mary Ellen Snodgrass

Wiley Publishing, Inc.

For general information on our other products and services or to obtain technical support please contact our Customer Care Department within the U.S. at (800) 762-2974, outside the U.S. at (317) 572-3993 or fax (317) 572-4002.

Wiley also publishes its books in a variety of electronic formats. Some content that appears in print may not be available in electronic books. For more information about Wiley products, please visit our web site at www.wiley.com.

Library of Congress Cataloging-in-Publication data is available from the publisher upon request.

ISBN 13: 978-0-0470-04154-3
ISBN 10: 0-470-04154-4

Printed in the United States of America

10 9 8 7 6 5 4 3 2 1

Book design by Melissa Auciello-Brogan
Book production by Wiley Publishing, Inc. Composition Services

Contents

ABOUT THE TRANSLATOR

Mary Ellen Snodgrass is an award-winning author of textbooks and general reference works, and a former columnist for the *Charlotte Observer*. A member of Phi Beta Kappa, she graduated magna cum laude from the University of North Carolina at Greensboro and Appalachian State University, and holds degrees in English, Latin, psychology, and the education of gifted children.

Introduction

*S*hakespeare on the Double! Romeo and Juliet provides the full text of the Bard's play side by side with an easy-to-read modern English translation that you can understand. You no longer have to wonder about the meaning of "What's in a name? That which we call a rose by any other name would smell as sweet"! You can read the Shakespearean text on the left-hand pages and check the right-hand pages when Shakespeare's language stumps you. Or you can read only the translation, which enables you to understand the action and characters, as an introduction to the Shakespearean English. You can also read both, referring easily between the original text and the modern translation. Any way you choose, you can now fully understand every line of the Bard's masterpiece!

We've also provided you with some additional resources:

- **Brief synopsis** of the plot and action provides a broad-strokes overview of the play.
- **Comprehensive character list** covers the actions, motivations, and characteristics of each major player.
- **Visual character map** displays who the major characters are and how they relate to each other.
- **Cycle-of-death** pinpoints the sequence of deaths in the play, including who dies, how they die, and why they die.
- **Reflective questions** help you delve even more into the themes and meanings of the play.

Reading Shakespeare can be slow and challenging. No more! With *Shakespeare on the Double! Romeo and Juliet,* you can read the play in language that you can grasp quickly and thoroughly.

Synopsis

ACT I

Prologue

At Verona, the chorus describes a lengthy blood-feud between the rival houses of Capulet and Montague. The prolonged enmity causes the deaths of two lovers. Their sacrifice is necessary to end the hostilities.

Scene 1

On a street in Verona, Capulet's servants, Gregory and Sampson, encounter Montague's men, Abraham and Balthasar. On the Montague side, Benvolio joins the fray with his sword raised. On the Capulet side, Tybalt follows Benvolio. Alerted to the street brawl, Capulet and his wife hurry to the scene. At Capulet's demand for a weapon, Prince Escalus halts the latest outbreak of the lengthy feud. He condemns to death the next citizen who breaches the peace. The prince summons Montague to court that afternoon in Old Freetown and arranges a meeting with Capulet. Meanwhile, Lady Montague frets over her son Romeo's unhappiness. Benvolio recalls seeing Romeo wandering a grove west of Verona an hour before sunrise. Despondent and lovesick, Romeo arrives in Verona shortly after nine. Benvolio is unable to lift Romeo's spirits.

Scene 2

In a Verona street, Count Paris discusses with Capulet a betrothal with Capulet's 13-year-old daughter Juliet. Capulet hesitates to pledge so young a girl to matrimony, yet accepts Paris's proposal if Juliet concurs with the plans. Capulet invites Paris to a traditional feast at the Capulet house on Sunday evening. An illiterate servant carries the invitation to the guests' homes. The servant stops Benvolio and Romeo to help him decipher the guest list. Benvolio decides to put on a mask and intrude on the party. Still mooning over Rosaline, who is one of the guests, Romeo agrees to accompany Benvolio.

2

Scene 3

At the Capulet home, Lady Capulet and the nurse discuss with Juliet the marriage offer from Paris. The nurse reminisces over her years of tending Juliet, whom she nursed in infancy after the death of the nurse's daughter Susan. Juliet is not eager to marry, but she promises to study her suitor's face and behavior at the feast.

Scene 4

That night, Romeo follows Benvolio and their high-spirited friend Mercutio by torchlight to the Capulet house. Mercutio annoys Romeo with blather about Queen Mab, the fairy queen, who influences human dreams.

Scene 5

Friends and relatives of the Capulets dance at a ball and await a late-night banquet. Although Romeo is a Montague, Capulet welcomes him. Romeo falls instantly in love with Juliet. Her hostile cousin Tybalt threatens to attack Romeo for coming uninvited to the gathering. Capulet quiets Tybalt, his brother's son, reminding him that the host has the last word on invitations. Capulet recalls when he was young and went masked to amusements. Romeo, unaware of Juliet's identity, kisses her. Too late, he and Juliet learn that they are members of opposite sides of the feuding Capulets and Montagues.

ACT II

Prologue

The chorus reports that Romeo has given up his pursuit of Rosaline because he prefers Juliet. Unlike the dismissive Rosaline, Juliet is more affectionate and receptive of Romeo's courtship.

Scene 1

Before dawn the next morning, Romeo paces alongside the Capulet orchard. He avoids his friends, who ridicule his lovesickness. He climbs the wall to get a second look at Juliet.

Scene 2

Outside Juliet's room, Romeo hears her sighing with love for him. She regrets that they belong to feuding families. He moves close enough to reveal his presence. The two denounce their family connections and pledge mutual love.

Scene 3

At sunrise, a Franciscan priest, Friar Laurence, collects herbs. Romeo arrives to discuss his new love. The friar suspects that Romeo flits from one girl to another out of immaturity. Friar Laurence encourages the idea of Romeo's union with Juliet as a way to end the protracted feud between the Capulets and the Montagues.

Scene 4

On Monday morning, Romeo walks through Verona in an upbeat mood that puzzles Benvolio and Mercutio. Romeo makes plans with Juliet's nurse to get Juliet to Friar Laurence's cell for the wedding. As an excuse to see the Friar, Juliet will get permission from her parents to go to confession. The nurse, who has tended Juliet from birth, warns Romeo not to deceive or disappoint the girl. Romeo sends a rope ladder with the nurse.

Scene 5

At the Capulet orchard, Juliet anticipates the nurse, who has not returned by noon. The nurse, arriving breathless from her walk to town, informs Juliet that Romeo will marry her that afternoon at Friar Laurence's cell. The rope ladder will allow Romeo to unite with his wife at her room that night.

Scene 6

Romeo and Juliet meet a third time at Friar Laurence's cell. He hurriedly unites them in wedlock.

ACT III

Scene 1

Benvolio and Mercutio taunt Tybalt with his nickname, the "Prince of Cats." Tybalt strikes back. Because Romeo is now Tybalt's cousin by marriage, he stands between Tybalt and Mercutio. Aiming under Romeo's arm, Tybalt thrusts his sword into Mercutio. Mercutio, realizing that he is mortally wounded, curses the Capulet and Montague families. In a rage at the loss of Mercutio, Romeo kills Tybalt. The Capulets demand punishment for Tybalt's killer. Lady Capulet proposes that Prince Escalus execute Romeo. The prince chooses a merciful course by exiling Romeo from Verona.

Scene 2

When the nurse informs Juliet of the latest street fight, Juliet mourns for Tybalt, even though he had a reputation for provoking his enemies. Juliet sends the nurse with a ring for Romeo, who has retreated to Friar Laurence's cell.

Scene 3

Meanwhile, Romeo grieves over a banishment that will end his marriage to Juliet. The nurse urges Romeo to help Juliet recover from the loss of a dear cousin. The friar suggests that Romeo go to Mantua and wait until the friar can work out a solution. Balthasar, Romeo's servant, will carry messages from Friar Laurence to Mantua.

Scene 4

Concerned for his daughter's intense sorrow, Capulet sets the wedding for Thursday. He hopes that marriage to Count Paris will ease his daughter's bouts of weeping. When Juliet balks at the plan, her father demands that she report to St. Peter's Church at the appointed time.

Scene 5

At daylight on Tuesday, the bridal couple hear the song of a lark, a token of morning. Juliet tries to keep Romeo in her room, but he must leave for Mantua or else face arrest. Capulet, who doesn't suspect his daughter's secret marriage, orders her to prepare for a wedding with Paris. The nurse thinks that Paris is the better choice of mate for Juliet. Juliet retreats to the friar's cell for advice.

ACT IV

Scene 1

When Juliet reaches Friar Laurence's cell, she encounters Paris finalizing the wedding plans. She gives him no indication of her marriage to the recently exiled Romeo. After Paris leaves her to confess in privacy, she mourns the turn of events that separates her from her husband. The friar chooses a powerful herb to suppress Juliet's vital functions. By swallowing the herb that night, Juliet will seem dead. The Capulets will inter her body above ground in the family burial vault. The ruse gives the friar time enough to inform Romeo of Juliet's quandary and to summon Romeo back to Verona to rescue his wife.

Scene 2

The Capulets hurriedly prepare food and invite a few friends to the wedding. They scale back the usual marriage celebration out of respect for Tybalt's recent death. Juliet pretends to comply by selecting clothes for the wedding. Capulet decides to hold the wedding on Wednesday and resolves to stay up all night.

Scene 3

At bedtime, Juliet sends the nurse away and pretends to pray to ready her spirit for marriage. She swallows the herb and, fully clothed, swoons onto the bed.

Scene 4

On Wednesday morning, the Capulets send the nurse to call Juliet. Count Paris plans to awaken his bride and escort her to the ceremony.

Scene 5

The nurse finds Juliet lifeless and unresponsive. The Capulets, Paris, and the nurse mourn Juliet's sudden demise. Friar Laurence tells them to rejoice that Juliet is in heaven. He instructs the family to dress her corpse and to sprinkle rosemary as a symbol of remembrance. He implies that God is punishing them. Anticipating a free meal, the musicians shift from wedding music to funeral songs.

ACT V

Scene 1

When Balthasar arrives in Mantua, he breaks the news to Romeo that Juliet is dead and buried. Romeo breaks city laws by buying poison from a poor pharmacist for forty ducats. Romeo hurries from Mantua to Verona to kill himself beside Juliet's corpse.

Scene 2

Friar John reports to Friar Laurence that a local quarantine prevented the delivery of a message to Romeo at Mantua. Friar Laurence plans to send another letter to Romeo. Within hours of Juliet's awakening in the tomb, Friar Laurence hurries to the vault with tools to open it and set her free. He plans to conceal Juliet at his cell until Romeo can arrive from Mantua.

Scene 3

By torchlight, Paris and his page reach the Capulet vault, where Paris scatters flowers and fragrant water to honor his bride-to-be. When Romeo and Balthasar arrive, Paris hides in the shadows. In the gloom, Romeo does not recognize him. Paris accuses Romeo of killing Tybalt and, indirectly, causing Juliet's death from grief. Romeo is unwilling to kill Paris, but he can't avoid another duel. Paris collapses and requests burial near Juliet. Romeo realizes that he has killed Paris. Near Tybalt's draped corpse in the vault, Romeo finds Juliet inert, but still pink-lipped and rosy-cheeked. He embraces and kisses her, swallows the poison, and collapses.

Meanwhile, Paris's page alerts the night watch. Juliet awakens and finds Romeo dead from the poison. Friar Laurence decides to convey her to a convent, but she refuses to leave Romeo. When the watchmen approach the cemetery, Friar Laurence hurries away. Because Romeo has drunk all the poison, Juliet kisses his lips in hopes of finding a drop. She unsheathes his dagger and plunges it into her chest.

Summoned from their beds, Capulet, Lady Capulet, Montague, and Prince Escalus arrive at the tragic scene. Montague reports that his wife has died of grief for her banished son. Prince Escalus investigates the causes of the three deaths. The most inexplicable is Juliet, whom the families assumed had died two days before. Balthasar, Paris's page, and Friar Laurence testify to their knowledge of the three deaths. After reading the letter that Romeo wrote to his father, Prince Escalus blames Capulet and Montague for the family hostilities. The prince admits his own fault in allowing the feud to continue. In reference to his own loss of a kinsman, he exclaims that "all are punished." Montague grasps Capulet's hand and promises to commission a gold statue to honor Juliet for being a faithful wife to Romeo.

List of Characters

JULIET   The Capulet daughter. She is presented as a young and innocent adolescent, not yet 14 years old. Her youthfulness is stressed throughout the play to illustrate her progression from adolescence to maturity and to emphasize her position as a tragic heroine. Juliet's love for Romeo gives her the strength and courage to defy her parents and face death twice.

ROMEO   The Montague son, who is loved and respected in Verona. He is initially presented as a comic lover, with his inflated declarations of love for Rosaline. After meeting Juliet, he abandons his tendency to be a traditional, fashionable lover, and his language becomes intense, reflecting his genuine passion for Juliet. By avenging Mercutio's death, he sets in motion a chain of tragic events that culminate in suicide when he mistakenly believes Juliet to be dead.

MERCUTIO   Kinsman to the prince and friend of Romeo. His name comes from the word *mercury,* the element that flashes like his quick temper. Mercutio is bawdy and talkative. He tries to tease Romeo out of his melancholy frame of mind. He accepts Tybalt's challenge to defend Romeo's honor. His death precipitates Romeo's rage and revenge, and the stabbing of Tybalt.

TYBALT   The Capulet's nephew and Juliet's cousin. Tybalt is violent and hot-tempered, with a strong sense of honor. He challenges Romeo to a duel in response to Romeo's attending a Capulet party. His challenge to Romeo incites Mercutio, whom Tybalt stabs. Romeo then kills Tybalt.

THE NURSE   Juliet's nursemaid. Since the death of her daughter Susan in infancy, the nurse has acted as confidante for Juliet. She later acts as a messenger between Juliet and Romeo. Like Mercutio, the Nurse loves to talk and reminisce, and her attitude toward love is bawdy. The Nurse is loving and affectionate toward Juliet, but compromises her position of trust when she advises Juliet to forget Romeo and comply with her parents' wishes for her to marry Paris.

FRIAR LAURENCE   A brother of the Franciscan order and Romeo's confessor, who advises both Romeo and Juliet. The Friar agrees to marry the couple in secret in the hope that marriage will restore peace between their families. His plans to reunite Juliet with Romeo go awry. The Friar concocts the potion plot through which Juliet appears dead for 42 hours in order to avoid marrying Paris. At the end of the play, the Prince recognizes the Friar's good intentions.

LORD CAPULET   Juliet's father is quick-tempered and impetuous but is initially reluctant to consent to Juliet's marriage with Paris because Juliet is so young. Later, he changes his mind and angrily demands that Juliet obey his wishes. The deaths of Romeo and Juliet reconcile Capulet with his enemy Montague.

PARIS   A noble young kinsman to the Prince. Paris is well-mannered and attractive and eager to marry Juliet. Romeo fights and kills Paris at the Capulet tomb when Paris assumes that Romeo has come to desecrate the bodies of Tybalt and Juliet.

BENVOLIO   Montague's nephew and a friend of Romeo and Mercutio. Benvolio is the peacemaker who attempts to halt strife between Tybalt and Mercutio. After the deaths of Mercutio and Tybalt, Benvolio acts as a chorus, explaining how the events took place.

LADY CAPULET   A loving but controlling parent. She demands Romeo's death for killing Tybalt. In her relationship with Juliet, she is cold and distant, expecting Juliet to obey her father and marry Paris.

LORD MONTAGUE   Romeo's father, who worries about his son's melancholy behavior. In a single night, he loses both his wife and son, and pledges a statue to his dead daughter-in-law.

BALTHASAR   Romeo's servant. He brings Romeo the news in Mantua that Juliet is dead.

AN APOTHECARY   A poverty-stricken chemist, who sells poison to Romeo in violation of the laws of Mantua.

ESCALUS, PRINCE OF VERONA   Although the symbol of law and order in Verona, he fails to quell the violence between the Montagues and Capulets. Only the deaths of Romeo and Juliet, rather than the authority of the prince, restore peace.

FRIAR JOHN   A brother of the Franciscan order, sent by Friar Laurence to tell Romeo of his sleeping potion plan for Juliet. A quarantine prevents the Friar from delivering the message to Romeo in Mantua.

LADY MONTAGUE   In contrast with Lady Capulet, Lady Montague dislikes the violence of the feud. Like her husband, she is concerned by her son's withdrawn and secretive behavior. The news of Romeo's banishment breaks her heart. She dies of grief.

PETER   A Capulet servant attending the nurse.

ABRAM   A servant to Montague.

SAMPSON   A boastful, posturing servant of the Capulet household.

GREGORY   Servant of the Capulet household who admires Sampson's brave talk.

Character Map

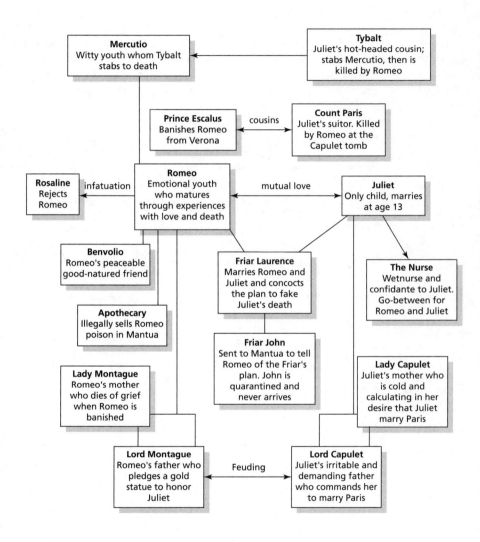

Mercutio
Witty youth whom Tybalt stabs to death

Tybalt
Juliet's hot-headed cousin; stabs Mercutio, then is killed by Romeo

Prince Escalus
Banishes Romeo from Verona

cousins

Count Paris
Juliet's suitor. Killed by Romeo at the Capulet tomb

Rosaline
Rejects Romeo

infatuation

Romeo
Emotional youth who matures through experiences with love and death

mutual love

Juliet
Only child, marries at age 13

Benvolio
Romeo's peaceable good-natured friend

Friar Laurence
Marries Romeo and Juliet and concocts the plan to fake Juliet's death

The Nurse
Wetnurse and confidante to Juliet. Go-between for Romeo and Juliet

Apothecary
Illegally sells Romeo poison in Mantua

Friar John
Sent to Mantua to tell Romeo of the Friar's plan. John is quarantined and never arrives

Lady Capulet
Juliet's mother who is cold and calculating in her desire that Juliet marry Paris

Lady Montague
Romeo's mother who dies of grief when Romeo is banished

Lord Montague
Romeo's father who pledges a gold statue to honor Juliet

Feuding

Lord Capulet
Juliet's irritable and demanding father who commands her to marry Paris

Cycle of Death

At its simplest, *Romeo and Juliet* is a play about finding true love in a world filled with conflict. This conflict is due to the Capulet and Montague families' ongoing feud, which is the impetus for the cycle of death throughout the play. The graphic below outlines the sequence of threatened, false, and real deaths that spur the plot.

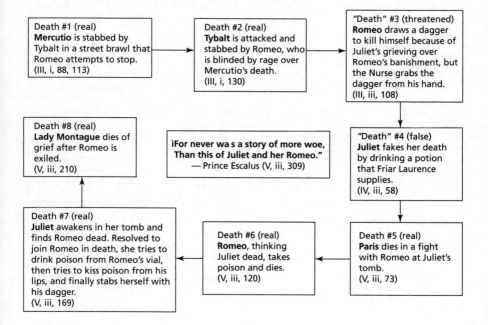

Death #1 (real)
Mercutio is stabbed by Tybalt in a street brawl that Romeo attempts to stop. (III, i, 88, 113)

Death #2 (real)
Tybalt is attacked and stabbed by Romeo, who is blinded by rage over Mercutio's death. (III, i, 130)

"Death" #3 (threatened)
Romeo draws a dagger to kill himself because of Juliet's grieving over Romeo's banishment, but the Nurse grabs the dagger from his hand. (III, iii, 108)

Death #8 (real)
Lady Montague dies of grief after Romeo is exiled. (V, iii, 210)

ïFor never wa s a story of more woe, Than this of Juliet and her Romeo."
— Prince Escalus (V, iii, 309)

"Death" #4 (false)
Juliet fakes her death by drinking a potion that Friar Laurence supplies. (IV, iii, 58)

Death #7 (real)
Juliet awakens in her tomb and finds Romeo dead. Resolved to join Romeo in death, she tries to drink poison from Romeo's vial, then tries to kiss poison from his lips, and finally stabs herself with his dagger. (V, iii, 169)

Death #6 (real)
Romeo, thinking Juliet dead, takes poison and dies. (V, iii, 120)

Death #5 (real)
Paris dies in a fight with Romeo at Juliet's tomb. (V, iii, 73)

Shakespeare's
Romeo and Juliet

ACT I, PROLOGUE

[Enter Chorus]

CHORUS   Two households, both alike in dignity,
      In fair Verona, where we lay our scene
From ancient grudge break to new mutiny,
      Where civil blood makes civil hands unclean.
From forth the fatal loins of these two foes   5
      A pair of star-crossed lovers take their life;
Whose misadventured piteous overthrows
      Doth with their death bury their parents' strife.
The fearful passage of their death-marked love,
      And the continuance of their parents' rage,   10
Which, but their children's end, naught could remove,
      Is now the two hours' traffic of our stage;
The which if you with patient ears attend,
What here shall miss, our toil shall strive to mend.
[Exeunt]

ACT I, PROLOGUE

[Narrator enters]

CHORUS   At Verona in north-central Italy, two noble families
reignite their grudge war. From these warring families
come a pair of doomed lovers who kill themselves. Their
sacrifice brings an end to the constant strife between
these families. Our two-hour play describes the pathetic
end to this love story, which in this case was the only
remedy for family warfare. Listen to this story.
[The narrator goes out]

ACT I, SCENE 1

Verona, a public place.

[Enter SAMPSON and GREGORY, with swords and bucklers, of the house of Capulet]

SAMPSON	Gregory, on my word, we'll not carry coals.
GREGORY	No, for then we should be colliers.
SAMPSON	I mean, an we be in choler, we'll draw.
GREGORY	Ay, while you live, draw your neck out of collar.

SAMPSON   I strike quickly, being moved.   5

GREGORY   But thou are not quickly moved to strike.

SAMPSON   A dog of the house of Montague moves me.

GREGORY   To move is to stir, and to be valiant is to stand.
Therefore, if thou art moved, thou runn'st away.

SAMPSON   A dog of that house shall move me to stand. I   10
will take the wall of any man or maid of Montague's.

GREGORY   That shows thee a weak slave; for the weakest
goes to the wall.

SAMPSON   'Tis true; and therefore women, being the
weaker vessels, are ever thrust to the wall. Therefore I   15
will push Montague's men from the wall and thrust
his maids to the wall.

GREGORY   The quarrel is between our masters, and us
their men.

SAMPSON   'Tis all one. I will show myself a tyrant. When   20
I have fought with the men, I will be cruel with the
maids—I will cut off their heads.

GREGORY   The heads of the maids?

SAMPSON   Ay, the heads of the maids, or their
maidenheads. Take it in what sense thou wilt.   25

GREGORY   They must take it in sense that feel it.

SAMPSON   Me they shall feel while I am able to stand;
and 'tis known I am a pretty piece of flesh.

ORIGINAL

ACT I, SCENE 1

A public gathering place in Verona.

[Entering are SAMPSON and GREGORY, two servants of the Capulet family armed with swords and small shields]

SAMPSON	Gregory, we won't tolerate insults by carrying coal.
GREGORY	No. If we carried coal, we would be coal dealers.
SAMPSON	I mean, if we are angered, we will draw our weapons.
GREGORY	Yes, while you are alive, you raise your neck from your collar.
SAMPSON	When I am stirred to action, I strike quickly.
GREGORY	But you aren't often aroused to anger.
SAMPSON	Any brute from the Montague house maddens me.
GREGORY	If you are aroused, you are stirred. If you are brave, you stand up to the enemy. But if you feel moved, you run away.
SAMPSON	I'll face any Montague brute as the enemy. I'll go to the wall with any man or woman in Montague's household.
GREGORY	Then you are a puny slave. The weakest man is pushed to the wall.
SAMPSON	You're right. And women, the weaker sex, are always getting pushed up against the wall. Therefore, I will press Montague's men away from the wall and force his women against the wall.
GREGORY	The feud is between noblemen. We servants do the fighting.
SAMPSON	It's all the same. I will display my courage. When I have fought off the Montague men, I will terrify the women— I will chop off their heads.
GREGORY	The heads of the women?
SAMPSON	Yes, the heads of the women, or their virginity. Interpret it any way you want.
GREGORY	The women must interpret whatever they feel.
SAMPSON	The women shall feel me when I stand up; I have a reputation for being well-built.

GREGORY	'Tis well thou art not fish; if thou hadst, thou hadst been poor-John. Draw thy tool! Here comes two of the house of Montagues. *[Enter two other Servingmen, ABRAM and BALTHASAR]*
SAMPSON	My naked weapon is out. Quarrel! I will back thee.
GREGORY	How? turn thy back and run?
SAMPSON	Fear me not.
GREGORY	No, marry. I fear thee!
SAMPSON	Let us take the law of our sides; let them begin.
GREGORY	I will frown as I pass by, and let them take it as they list.
SAMPSON	Nay, as they dare. I will bite my thumb at them, which is disgrace to them if they bear it.
ABRAM	Do you bite your thumb at us, sir?
SAMPSON	I do bite my thumb, Sir.
ABRAM	Do you bite your thumb at us, sir?
SAMPSON	*[Aside to GREGORY]* Is the law of our side if I say ay?
GREGORY	*[Aside to SAMPSON]* No.
SAMPSON	No, sir, I do not bite my thumb at you, sir; but I bite my thumb, sir.
GREGORY	Do you quarrel, sir?
ABRAM	Quarrel, sir? No, sir.
SAMPSON	But if you do, sir, I am for you. I serve as good a man as you.
ABRAM	No better.
SAMPSON	Well, sir. *[Enter BENVOLIO]*
GREGORY	*[Aside to SAMPSON]* Say 'better.' Here comes one of my master's kinsmen.
SAMPSON	Yes, better, sir.
ABRAM	You lie.

30

35

40

45

50

55

GREGORY	It is good that you aren't a fish. If you had been a fish, you would have been a shriveled salted hake. Draw your sword! Here come two servants of the Montague family. *[Entering are two servants, ABRAM and BALTHASAR]*
SAMPSON	My sword is out of its sheath. Start the fight. I will back you up.
GREGORY	How? By turning and running?
SAMPSON	Don't worry about me.
GREGORY	No, indeed. I fear you!
SAMPSON	Let's defend our side. Let them start the fight.
GREGORY	I will scowl at them as I go by and let them respond however they want.
SAMPSON	No, let them take it as they dare. I will bite my thumb as an insult to them.
ABRAM	Are you biting your thumb at us, sir?
SAMPSON	Yes, I am biting my thumb, sir.
ABRAM	Do you bite your thumb at us, sir?
SAMPSON	*[In private to GREGORY]* Is it legal if I say yes?
GREGORY	*[In private to SAMPSON]* No.
SAMPSON	No, sir, I am not biting my thumb at you, sir, but I am biting my thumb, sir.
GREGORY	Do you want a fight, sir?
ABRAM	A fight, sir? No, sir.
SAMPSON	But if you do want a fight, sir, I will attack you. I serve as worthy a master as you do.
ABRAM	Your master is no better than mine.
SAMPSON	I see, sir. *[Enter BENVOLIO]*
GREGORY	*[Privately, to SAMPSON]* Say our master is better. Here comes a relative of the Capulets.
SAMPSON	Yes, my master is better, sir.
ABRAM	You are lying.

SAMPSON	Draw, if you be men. Gregory remember thy swashing blow. 60 *[They fight]*
BENVOLIO	Part, fools! Put up your swords. You know not what you do. *[Enter TYBALT]*
TYBALT	What, art thou drawn among these heartless hinds? Turn thee, Benvolio! look upon thy death.
BENVOLIO	I do but keep the peace. Put up thy sword, 65 Or manage it to part these men with me.
TYBALT	What, drawn, and talk of peace? I hate the word, As I hate hell, all Montagues, and thee. Have at thee, coward! *[They fight]* *[Enter an Officer, and three or four Citizens with clubs or partisans]*
OFFICER	Clubs, bills, and partisans! Strike! Beat them down! 70
CITIZENS	Down with the Capulets! Down with the Montagues! *[Enter old CAPULET in his gown, and his Wife]*
CAPULET	What noise is this? Give me my long sword, ho!
WIFE	A crutch, a crutch! Why call you for a sword?
CAPULET	My sword, I say! Old Montague is come 75 And flourishes his blade in spite of me. *[Enter old MONTAGUE and his Wife]*
MONTAGUE	Thou villain Capulet!—Hold me not, let me go.
MONTAGUE'S WIFE	Thou shalt not stir one foot to seek a foe. *[Enter PRINCE ESCALUS, with his Train]*

SAMPSON	Draw your swords, if you are real men. Gregory, remember your killer slice. *[They fight]*
BENVOLIO	Stop, fools! Put up your swords. You don't know how dangerous this is. *[Enter TYBALT]*
TYBALT	What is this? Are you attacking these weakling cowards? Turn, Benvolio! Face your death.
BENVOLIO	I am trying to make peace. Put up your sword, or use it to help me stop this fight.
TYBALT	You aim your sword and talk about peace? I hate peace as I hate hell, the Montague family, and you. I challenge you, coward! *[They fight] [Entering are a Peace Officer and three or four Citizens of Verona with clubs and spears]*
OFFICER	Clubs, axes, and spears! Attack! Beat them down!
CITIZENS	Down with the Capulets! Down with the Montagues! *[Entering are the elder CAPULET in his dressing gown and his Wife]*
CAPULET	What is this disturbance? Hand me my military sword!
WIFE	Bring him a crutch! Why are you demanding a sword?
CAPULET	I want my sword! The elder Montague is here and is waving his weapon in my face. *[Entering are old MONTAGUE and his Wife]*
MONTAGUE	You criminal Capulet!—Don't stop me. Let me at him.
MONTAGUE'S WIFE	You won't take one step toward an enemy. *[PRINCE ESCALUS enters with his followers]*

ACT I

PRINCE   Rebellious subjects, enemies to peace,
Profaners of this neighbor-stained steel—   80
Will they not hear? What, ho! you men, you beasts,
That quench the fire of your pernicious rage
With purple fountains issuing from your veins!
On pain of torture, from those bloody hands
Throw your mistempered weapons to the ground   85
And hear the sentence of your moved prince.
Three civil brawls, bred of an airy word
By thee, old Capulet, and Montague,
Have thrice disturbed the quiet of our streets
And made Verona's ancient citizens   90
Cast by their grave beseeming ornaments
To wield old partisans, in hands as old,
Cank'red with peace, to part your cank'red hate.
If ever you disturb our streets again,
Your lives shall pay the forfeit of the peace.   95
For this time all the rest depart away.
You, Capulet, shall go along with me;
And, Montague, come you this afternoon,
To know our farther pleasure in this case,
To old Freetown, our common judgment place.   100
Once more, on pain of death, all men depart.
[Exeunt all but MONTAGUE, his Wife, and BENVOLIO]

MONTAGUE   Who set this ancient quarrel new abroach?
Speak, nephew, were you by when it began?

BENVOLIO   Here were the servants of your adversary
And yours, close fighting ere I did approach.   105
I drew to part them. In the instant came
The fiery Tybalt, with his sword prepared;
Which, as he breathed defiance to my ears,
He swung about his head and cut the winds,
Who, nothing hurt withal, hissed him in scorn.   110
While we were interchanging thrusts and blows,
Came more and more, and fought on part and part,
Till the Prince came, who parted either part.

MONTAGUE'S
WIFE   O, where is Romeo? Saw you him today?
Right glad I am he was not at this fray.   115

PRINCE | Rebels, disturbers of the peace, slayers of neighbors, will you not listen to me? Are you animals venting your anger with blood-letting? I will have you tortured if you don't drop your weapons and listen to the punishment for feuding. Three times, Capulet and Montague, your feud has disturbed Verona and forced citizens to take up spears to halt the fighting. If your feud disturbs the peace again, you will die for it. Once more, on pain of death, all men depart. Capulet, come with me. Montague, you come this afternoon to Freetown, our courtroom, to hear my solution to this fighting. Finally, everyone clear the streets or die. *[All depart except for MONTAGUE, his Wife, and BENVOLIO]*

MONTAGUE | Who started this new episode of fighting? Tell me, nephew, were you here when it began?

BENVOLIO | Your enemy's servants and your men were already fighting when I arrived. I drew my sword to separate them. Immediately, the hot-tempered Tybalt drew his sword. While he shouted defiance, he swung his sword overhead, sliced the air, and did no more damage than make a swish. While we were clashing with our swords, more men joined the fray. Then Prince Escalus arrived and forced an end to the attack.

MONTAGUE'S WIFE | Where is Romeo? Have you seen him today? I am glad he wasn't involved in the fight.

TRANSLATION

BENVOLIO	Madam, an hour before the worshipped sun Peered forth the golden window of the East, A troubled mind drave me to walk abroad; Where, underneath the grove of sycamore That westward rooteth from this city side, 120 So early walking did I see your son. Towards him I made, but he was ware of me And stole into the covert of the wood. I, measuring his affections by my own, Which then most sought where most might not be found, 125 Being one too many by my weary self, Pursued my humor, not pursuing his, And gladly shunned who gladly fled from me.
MONTAGUE	Many a morning hath he there been seen, With tears augmenting the fresh morning's dew, 130 Adding to clouds more clouds with his deep sighs; But all so soon as the all-cheering sun Should in the farthest East begin to draw The shady curtains from Aurora's bed, Away from light steals home my heavy son 135 And private in his chamber pens himself, Shuts up his windows, locks fair daylight out, And makes himself an artificial night. Black and portentous must this humor prove Unless good counsel may the cause remove. 140
BENVOLIO	My noble uncle, do you know the cause?
MONTAGUE	I neither know it nor can learn of him.
BENVOLIO	Have you importuned him by any means?
MONTAGUE	Both by myself and many other friends; But he, his own affections' counsellor, 145 Is to himself—I will not say how true— But to himself so secret and so close, So far from sounding and discovery, As is the bud bit with an envious worm Ere he can spread his sweet leaves to the air 150 Or dedicate his beauty to the sun. Could we but learn from whence his sorrows grow, We would as willingly give cure as know. *[Enter ROMEO]*

BENVOLIO   Madam Montague, an hour before sunrise, I eased my troubled thoughts with a pre-dawn walk. I saw your son in a sycamore grove on the west side of Verona. I walked toward him, but he saw me coming and crept into the woods. Realizing that he wanted to be alone like me, I did not follow him.

MONTAGUE   He spends many mornings in the grove weeping and sighing. As soon as the sun rises, my troubled son shuts himself in his room, closes the shutters over the windows, and retreats into the dark. His mood must remain dark and ominous until good advice lightens it.

BENVOLIO   Uncle Montague, why is Romeo so moody?

MONTAGUE   I don't know, and he won't tell me.

BENVOLIO   Have you asked him?

MONTAGUE   My friends and I have tried. He keeps his feelings private and remains quiet and apart from us. He acts like a flower bud that has a worm chewing on its interior before it can blossom. If we could learn the cause of his grief, we would look for a remedy. *[Enter ROMEO]*

BENVOLIO	See, where he comes. So please you step aside,
	I'll know his grievance, or be much denied. 155
MONTAGUE	I would thou wert so happy by thy stay
	To hear true shrift. Come, madam, let's away.
	[Exeunt MONTAGUE, and Wife]
BENVOLIO	Good morrow, cousin.
ROMEO	Is the day so young?
BENVOLIO	But new struck nine. 160
ROMEO	Ay me! sad hours seem long.
	Was that my father that went hence so fast?
BENVOLIO	It was. What sadness lengthens Romeo's hours?
ROMEO	Not having that which having makes them short.
BENVOLIO	In love?
ROMEO	Out—
BENVOLIO	Of love? 165
ROMEO	Out of her favor where I am in love.
BENVOLIO	Alas that love, so gentle in his view,
	Should be so tyrannous and rough in proof!
ROMEO	Alas that love, whose view is muffled still,
	Should without eyes see pathways to his will! 170
	Where shall we dine? O me! What fray was here?
	Yet tell me not, for I have heard it all.
	Here's much to do with hate, but more with love.
	Why then, O brawling love, O loving hate,
	O anything, of nothing first create! 175
	O heavy lightness, serious vanity,
	Misshapen chaos of well-seeming forms,
	Feather of lead, bright smoke, cold fire, sick health,
	Still-waking sleep, that is not what it is!
	This love feel I, that feel no love in this. 180
	Dost thou not laugh?
BENVOLIO	No, coz, I rather weep.
ROMEO	Good heart, at what?
BENVOLIO	At thy good heart's oppression.

ORIGINAL

BENVOLIO	Here he comes. Leave us alone. I'll find out his problem or make him give me reasons for his refusal.
MONTAGUE	I wish you could be as rewarded in meeting with Romeo as you would be at holy confession. Come, Madam, let's go. *[MONTAGUE and his Wife depart]*
BENVOLIO	Good morning, cousin.
ROMEO	Is it still morning?
BENVOLIO	It's 9:00 A.M.
ROMEO	Sadness makes the hours drag. Was that my father who just hurried away?
BENVOLIO	It was. What is making you so sad, Romeo?
ROMEO	I am sad because I can't have what I want.
BENVOLIO	Are you in love?
ROMEO	Out—
BENVOLIO	Out of love?
ROMEO	Out of favor with my beloved.
BENVOLIO	It is unfortunate that love is gentle on first appearance, but that it becomes demanding and harsh in reality.
ROMEO	It is unfortunate that Cupid, who is blind, manages to see where he wants to go. Where shall we eat lunch? What fight happened here? Better yet, don't tell me. I've heard it all before. Verona is too involved in hate and not involved enough with love. Why does love quarrel and hate without doing some good! Oh clashing emotions that keep me awake, this is not love! This feeling lacks real affection. Don't you think it's funny?
BENVOLIO	No, cousin, I think it's sad.
ROMEO	Why do you weep?
BENVOLIO	At the harm done to a loving heart.

ACT 1

TRANSLATION

ROMEO	Why, such is love's transgression.
	Griefs of mine own lie heavy in my breast,
	Which thou wilt propagate, to have it prest 185
	With more of thine. This love that thou hast shown
	Doth add more grief to too much of mine own.
	Love is a smoke raised with the fume of sighs;
	Being purged, a fire sparkling in lovers' eyes;
	Being vexed, a sea nourished with lovers' tears. 190
	What is it else? A madness most discreet,
	A choking gall, and a preserving sweet.
	Farewell, my coz.
BENVOLIO	Soft! I will go along.
	An if you leave me so, you do me wrong.
ROMEO	Tut! I have lost myself; I am not here; 195
	This is not Romeo, he's some other where.
BENVOLIO	Tell me in sadness, who is that you love?
ROMEO	What, shall I groan and tell thee?
BENVOLIO	Groan? Why, no;
	But sadly tell me who.
ROMEO	Bid a sick man in sadness make his will. 200
	Ah, word ill urged to one that is so ill!
	In sadness, cousin, I do love a woman.
BENVOLIO	I aimed so near when I supposed you loved.
ROMEO	A right good markman. And she's fair I love.
BENVOLIO	A right fair mark, fair coz, is soonest hit. 205
ROMEO	Well, in that hit you miss. She'll not be hit
	With Cupid's arrow. She hath Dian's wit,
	And, in strong proof of chastity well armed,
	From Love's weak childish bow she lives unharmed.
	She will not stay the siege of loving terms, 210
	Nor bide th' encounter of assailing eyes,
	Nor ope her lap to saint-seducing gold.
	O, she is rich in beauty; only poor
	That, when she dies, with beauty dies her store.
BENVOLIO	Then she hath sworn that she will live chaste? 215

ROMEO	That is love's fault. My heavy grief will grow heavier if I have made you sad. Your concern for me makes me sadder. Romance is just vapor that comes from sighing and weeping, the result of lost affection and impatience. What else is love? It is a secret insanity, a choking bitterness in the throat, and a sweetness that makes it continue. 'Bye, cousin.
BENVOLIO	I will go with you. If you leave me in this sad mood, you wrong me.
ROMEO	I am lost in my thoughts. I am not here. The real Romeo is somewhere else.
BENVOLIO	Tell me sad and straight, whom do you love?
ROMEO	Do you want me to groan out her name?
BENVOLIO	No. Don't groan. Tell me her name.
ROMEO	If you ask a sick man to write his will, the request comes at a bad time. Cousin, I love a woman.
BENVOLIO	I already guessed that.
ROMEO	You hit a bull's-eye. And she's pretty.
BENVOLIO	A pretty girl, my cousin, is the first target.
ROMEO	In that, you are wrong. She dodges Cupid's arrow. She is as witty as Diana, the goddess of chastity. She protects her virginity. She lives free of infatuation. She won't listen to sweet talk. She avoids moony glances. She rejects bribes. She is beautiful. If she died young, beauty would expire with her, leaving her poor.
BENVOLIO	Has she vowed to remain a virgin?

ROMEO	She hath, and in that sparing makes huge waste;
	For beauty, starved with her severity,
	Cuts beauty off from all posterity.
	She is too fair, too wise, wisely too fair,
	To merit bliss by making me despair. 220
	She hath forsworn to love, and in that vow
	Do I live dead that live to tell it now.
BENVOLIO	Be ruled by me; forget to think of her.
ROMEO	O, teach me how I should forget to think!
BENVOLIO	By giving liberty unto thine eyes. 225
	Examine other beauties.
ROMEO	'Tis the way
	To call hers (exquisite) in question more.
	These happy masks that kiss fair ladies' brows,
	Being black puts us in mind they hide the fair.
	He that is strucken blind cannot forget 230
	The precious treasure of his eyesight lost.
	Show me a mistress that is passing fair,
	What doth her beauty serve but as a note
	Where I may read who passed that passing fair?
	Farewell. Thou canst not teach me to forget. 235
BENVOLIO	I'll pay that doctrine, or else die in debt.
	[Exeunt]

ROMEO	She has. It is such a waste. A beautiful woman who remains a virgin halts the transfer of her beauty to her children. She is too beautiful, too wise, and undeserving of respect for making me unhappy. She has sworn off romance. Because of that promise, I might as well be dead.

BENVOLIO	Listen to me: forget her.
ROMEO	Show me how I can escape my thoughts!
BENVOLIO	Free yourself from her. Look at other girls.
ROMEO	If I do, comparisons will make her seem even more exquisite. These fashionable masks that pretty women wear hide beauty under a black surface. The man who is blinded can't forget the beauty that he once could see. Show me a pretty woman. Her looks are a reminder of my love, who outshines ordinary loveliness. Goodbye. You fail to make me forget her.
BENVOLIO	I'll ease your sorrow or die trying. *[They go out]*

ACT I, SCENE 2

The same. A street.

[Enter CAPULET, COUNTY PARIS, and a Servant]

CAPULET	But Montague is bound as well as I,
	In penalty alike; and 'tis not hard, I think,
	For men so old as we to keep the peace.
PARIS	Of honorable reckoning are you both,
	And pity 'tis you lived at odds so long. 5
	But now, my lord, what say you to my suit?
CAPULET	But saying o'er what I have said before:
	My child is yet a stranger in the world,
	She hath not seen the change of fourteen years;
	Let two more summers wither in their pride 10
	Ere we may think her ripe to be a bride.
PARIS	Younger than she are happy mothers made.
CAPULET	And too soon marred are those so early made.
	Earth hath swallowed all my hopes but she;
	She is the hopeful lady of my earth. 15
	But woo her, gentle Paris, get her heart;
	My will to her consent is but a part.
	An she agree, within her scope of choice
	Lies my consent and fair according voice.
	This night I hold an old accustomed feast, 20
	Whereto I have invited many a guest,
	Such as I love; and you among the store,
	One more, most welcome, makes my number more.
	At my poor house look to behold this night
	Earth-treading stars that make dark heaven light. 25
	Such comfort as do lusty young men feel
	When well-apparelled April on the heel
	Of limping Winter treads, even such delight
	Among fresh fennel buds shall you this night
	Inherit at my house. Hear all, all see, 30
	And like her most whose merit most shall be;
	Which, on more view of many, mine, being one,
	May stand in number, though in reck'ning none.
	Come, go with me.

ORIGINAL

ACT I, SCENE 2

A street in Verona.

[Entering are LORD CAPULET, COUNT PARIS, and a Servant]

CAPULET   Both Montague and I must stop the feud or be executed. It is not difficult for two old men to live peaceably.

PARIS   You are both worthy men. It is a shame you fought each other so long. As to your business, what do you think of my proposal?

CAPULET   I must repeat. My daughter is still a child, not yet fourteen years old. Wait two years before marrying her.

PARIS   Girls younger than she are already mothers.

CAPULET   Those who marry too soon are ruined. She is my only living child . . . my future hope. Court her, Paris, win her affection. I will agree to wed her to the man she loves. If she agrees to your proposal, I will consent to the engagement. Tonight I am holding a traditional dinner party for all my friends. You are invited. Among the guests you will see sparkling girls who make the sky seem dark. Young men feel romantic when April follows winter, and you will see such young beauties among my guests tonight. Look at all of them and choose the girl you like best. When you look at them all, my daughter may stand among them, but not catch your eye. Come with me.

[To Servant, giving him a paper]
             Go, sirrah, trudge about
Through fair Verona; find those persons out   35
Whose names are written there, and to them say,
My house and welcome on their pleasure stay.
[Exit, with PARIS]

SERVANT   Find them out whose names are written here?
It is written that the shoemaker should meddle with
his yard and the tailor with his last, the fisher with his   40
pencil and the painter with his nets; but I am sent to
find those persons whose names are here writ, and can
never find what names the writing person hath here
writ. I must to the learned. In good time!
[Enter BENVOLIO and ROMEO]

BENVOLIO   Tut, man, one fire burns out another's burning;   **45**
One pain is less'ned by another's anguish;
Turn giddy, and be holp by backward turning;
One desperate grief cures with another's languish.
Take thou some new infection to thy eye,
And the rank poison of the old will die.   50

ROMEO   Your plantain leaf is excellent for that.

BENVOLIO   For what, I pray thee?

ROMEO   For your broken shin.

BENVOLIO   Why, Romeo, art thou mad?

ROMEO   Not mad, but bound more than a madman is;
Shut up in prison, kept without my food,   55
Whipped and tormented and—God-den, good fellow.

SERVANT   God gi' go-den. I pray, sir, can you read?

ROMEO   Ay, mine own fortune in my misery.

SERVANT   Perhaps you have learned it without book.
But I pray, can you read anything you see?   60

ROMEO   Ay, if I know the letters and the language.

SERVANT   Ye say honestly. Rest you merry.

[To Servant, giving him a paper] You, servant, walk through Verona. Locate the people on this list and invite them to my house. *[CAPULET goes out with PARIS]*

SERVANT Locate the people listed here? Cobblers measure cloth, tailors mold shoes, fishers draw with a pencil, and painters cast nets. I must locate the people listed here, but I can't read the names. I must locate someone who can read. Eventually I will finish my errand! *[Enter BENVOLIO and ROMEO]*

BENVOLIO Hush, Romeo. A new romance can consume the old fires of love. Your pain will give way to new passion. Be light-hearted and turn your back on the old love. A new passionate love will cure your moping. Get a new girlfriend and the memory of the old girlfriend will wither away in your mind.

ROMEO The weed called dock is an excellent remedy.

BENVOLIO For what?

ROMEO For a broken leg.

BENVOLIO Are you crazy, Romeo?

ROMEO Not crazy, but locked up like a madman—shut in a cell, starved, whipped, and tortured. *[To CAPULET's servant]* Good day, friend.

SERVANT Good day to you. Please, can you read?

ROMEO Yes, I can read my fate in my misery.

SERVANT It's possible to learn your destiny without books. Please, can you read what you see?

ROMEO Yes, if I know the alphabet and language.

SERVANT You speak the truth. Fare you well.

TRANSLATION

ROMEO	Stay, fellow; I can read.
	[He reads the letter]
	'Signior Martino and his wife and daughters;
	County Anselmo and his beauteous sisters; 65
	The lady widow of Vitruvio;
	Signior Placentio and his lovely nieces;
	Mercutio and his brother Valentine;
	Mine uncle Capulet, his wife, and daughters;
	My fair niece Rosaline and Livia; 70
	Signior Valentio and his cousin Tybalt;
	Lucio and the lively Helena.'
	A fair assembly. Whither should they come?
SERVANT	Up.
ROMEO	Whither? To supper? 75
SERVANT	To our house.
ROMEO	Whose house?
SERVANT	My master's.
ROMEO	Indeed I should have asked you that before.
SERVANT	Now I'll tell you without asking. My master is 80
	the great rich Capulet; and if you be not of the house
	of Montagues, I pray come and crush a cup of wine.
	Rest you merry.
	[Exit]
BENVOLIO	At this same ancient feast of Capulet's
	Sups the fair Rosaline whom thou so loves; 85
	With all the admired beauties of Verona.
	Go thither, and with unattainted eye
	Compare her face with some that I shall show,
	And I will make thee think thy swan a crow.
ROMEO	When the devout religion of mine eye 90
	Maintains such falsehood, then turn tears to fires;
	And these, who, often drowned, could never die,
	Transparent heretics, be burnt for liars!
	One fairer than my love? The all-seeing sun
	Ne'er saw her match since first the world begun. 95

ROMEO	Wait. I can read. *[He reads the letter]* Mr. Martino, his wife, and his daughters; Count Anselmo and his beautiful sisters; Vitruvio's widow; Mr. Placentio and his lovely nieces; Mercutio and his brother Valentine; My uncle Capulet, his wife, and their daughters; My pretty niece Rosaline and Livia; Mr. Valentio and his cousin Tybalt; Lucio and the high-spirited Helena. A good guest list. Where are they invited?
SERVANT	Up.
ROMEO	Where? To dinner?
SERVANT	To our house.
ROMEO	Whose house?
SERVANT	My master's house.
ROMEO	I should have asked that first.
SERVANT	I will explain it all. My master is the wealthy Capulet. If you aren't a Montague, I invite you to come and down a cup of wine. Farewell. *[He goes out]*
BENVOLIO	Rosaline, your beloved, is invited to this traditional dinner that Capulet holds. All the beauties of Verona will be there. Go to the party and without prejudice compare her face to the girls I will point out. They will make your swan seem like a crow.
ROMEO	When my worshipping eyes are false to Rosaline, my tears will turn into passion. And these weeping eyes will never be executed for lying to me. Is there a girl prettier than Rosaline? The sun hasn't seen her equal since the beginning of time.

BENVOLIO   Tut! you saw her fair, none else being by,
Herself poised with herself in either eye;
But in that crystal scales let there be weighed
Your lady's love against some other maid
That I will show you shining at this feast,   100
And she shall scant show well that now seems best.

ROMEO   I'll go along, no such sight to be shown,
But to rejoice in splendor of my own. *[Exeunt]*

ORIGINAL

BENVOLIO   Hush. She seemed beautiful to you because you didn't have anyone to compare her to. She filled both your eyes. But, at this dinner, clearly weigh your admiration for Rosaline against your love for some other beauty. Rosaline will no longer seem the most beautiful.

ROMEO   I will go with you, but I won't find a prettier girl. I will have time to enjoy Rosaline's splendor. *[They go out]*

TRANSLATION

ACT I, SCENE 3

A room in Capulet's house.

[Enter CAPULET'S WIFE, and NURSE]

WIFE   Nurse, where's my daughter? Call her forth to me.

NURSE   Now, by my maidenhead at twelve year old,
I bade her come. What, lamb! What, ladybird!
God forbid. Where's this girl? What, Juliet!
[Enter JULIET]

JULIET   How now? Who calls?

NURSE   Your mother.   5

JULIET   Madam, I am here. What is your will?

WIFE   This is the matter—Nurse, give leave awhile,
We must talk in secret. Nurse, come back again;
I have rememb'red me, thou 's hear our counsel.
Thou knowest my daughter's of a pretty age.   10

NURSE   Faith, I can tell her age unto an hour.

WIFE   She's not fourteen.

NURSE   I'll lay fourteen of my teeth—
And yet, to my teen be it spoken, I have but four—
She's not fourteen. How long is it now
To Lammastide?

WIFE   A fortnight and odd days.   15

NURSE   Even or odd, of all days in the year,
Come Lammas Eve at night shall she be fourteen.
Susan and she (God rest all Christian souls!)
Were of an age. Well, Susan is with God;
She was too good for me. But, as I said,   20
On Lammas Eve at night shall she be fourteen;
That shall she, marry; I remember it well.
'Tis since the earthquake now eleven years;
And she was weaned (I never shall forget it),
Of all the days of the year, upon that day;   25

ACT I, SCENE 3

A room in Capulet's house.

[Entering are CAPULET'S WIFE and a NURSEMAID or chaperone]

WIFE	Nurse, where is my daughter? Call her here.
NURSE	I swear by my virginity at age twelve, I've already called her. Lamb, ladybird, where are you! God help us, where is she? Juliet, where are you! *[Enter JULIET]*
JULIET	What? Who wants me?
NURSE	Your mother.
JULIET	Madam, I am here. What do you want?
WIFE	This is what we must discuss—Nurse, give us privacy. We must talk in secret. Nurse, come back. I just remembered that you should hear my advice. You know my daughter is reaching a marriageable age.
NURSE	Indeed, I know her age down to the hour.
WIFE	She's not yet fourteen.
NURSE	I will wager fourteen of my teeth—even though I have only four—that she's not fourteen. How long is it until August 1?
WIFE	Two weeks and a few days.
NURSE	Whatever the count, of all the days on the calendar, on the evening of August 1, she will be fourteen. My Susan and Juliet (God rest Christian souls!) were the same age. Well, Susan died. She was too good for me. As I was saying, on the night of August 1, Juliet will be fourteen; Yes, she will. I remember it well. It's been eleven years since the earthquake happened, I weaned her—I shall never forget—the day of the quake.

TRANSLATION

For I had then laid wormwood to my dug,
Sitting in the sun under the dovehouse wall.
My lord and you were then at Mantua.
Nay, I do bear a brain. But, as I said,
When it did taste the wormwood on the nipple   30
Of my dug and felt it bitter, pretty fool,
To see it tetchy and fall out with the dug!
Shake, quoth the dovehouse! 'Twas no need, I trow,
To bid me trudge.
And since that time it is eleven years,   35
For then she could stand high-lone; nay, by th' rood,
She could have run and waddled all about;
For even the day before, she broke her brow;
And then my husband (God be with his soul!
'A was a merry man) took up the child.   40
'Yea,' quoth he, 'dost thou fall upon thy face?
Thou wilt fall backward when thou hast more wit;
Wilt thou not, Jule?' and, by my holidam,
The pretty wretch left crying and said 'Ay.'
To see now how a jest shall come about!   45
I warrant, an I should live a thousand years,
I never should forget it. 'Wilt thou not, Jule?' quoth he,
And, pretty fool, it stinted and said 'Ay.'

WIFE   Enough of this. I pray thee hold thy peace.

NURSE   Yes, madam. Yet I cannot choose but laugh   50
                To think it should leave crying and say 'Ay.'
                And yet, I warrant, it had upon it brow
                A bump as big as a young cock'rel's stone;
                A perilous knock; and it cried bitterly.
                'Yea,' quoth my husband, 'fall'st upon thy face? 55
                Thou wilt fall backward when thou comest to age;
                Wilt thou not, Jule?' It stinted and said 'Ay.'

JULIET   And stint thou too, I pray thee, nurse, say I.

NURSE   Peace, I have done. God mark thee to his grace;
                Thou wast the prettiest babe that e'er I nursed. 60
                An I might live to see thee married once,
                I have my wish.

WIFE   Marry, that 'marry' is the very theme
                I came to talk of. Tell me, daughter Juliet,
                How stands your disposition to be married?   65

JULIET   It is an honor that I dream not of.

Sitting in the sun next to the dovecote, I put bitter artemisia juice on my nipple. You and Lord Capulet had gone to Mantua. I do have a good memory. As I was saying, the child tasted the bitter juice on my nipple and fretted. The dovecote began to shake. I vow, nobody had to make me move away. And by that time eleven years ago, she could stand alone, run, and toddle about. The day before, she bumped her head. My husband (God keep his soul! He was a jolly man) picked her up. "Yes," he said, "did you fall on your face? You will tumble backward when you are older, won't you, Jule?" And the pretty child stopped crying and said "yes." To see how a joke can come true! I promise you, if I live a thousand years, I won't forget it. "Won't you, Jule?" he said, and, the pretty child, she stopped crying and said, "Yes."

WIFE   Quiet. Please, no more chatter.

NURSE   Yes, ma'am. But I can't stop laughing to think of her ceasing her cry and saying "Yes." And yet, I vow, she had a lump on her forehead as big as a young rooster's testicle. A dangerous fall and she cried bitterly. "Yes," said my husband, "did you fall on your face? You will fall on your back when you become a young woman. Won't you, Jule?" And she stopped crying and said, "Yes."

JULIET   Stop talking, please, nurse.

NURSE   Peace, I have said all I'm going to say. God grant you his goodness. You were the prettiest child that I ever nursed. I hope I may live long enough to see you married.

WIFE   Marriage is the topic I want to discuss. Tell me, Juliet, what do you think about being married?

JULIET   It is an honor that I have never thought about.

TRANSLATION

NURSE   An honor? Were not I thine only nurse,
               I would say thou hadst sucked wisdom from thy teat.

WIFE   Well, think of marriage now. Younger than you,
               Here in Verona, ladies of esteem,   70
               Are made already mothers. By my count,
               I was your mother much upon these years
               That you are now a maid. Thus then in brief:
               The valiant Paris seeks you for his love.

NURSE   A man, young lady! Lady, such a man   75
               As all the world—why he's a man of wax.

WIFE   Verona's summer hath not such a flower.

NURSE   Nay, he's a flower, in faith—a very flower.

WIFE   What say you? Can you love the gentleman?
               This night you shall behold him at our feast.   80
               Read o'er the volume of young Paris' face,
               And find delight writ there with beauty's pen,
               Examine every married lineament,
               And see how one another lends content;
               And what obscured in this fair volume lies   85
               Find written in the margent of his eyes.
               This precious book of love, this unbound lover,
               To beautify him only lacks a cover.
               The fish lives in the sea, and 'tis much pride
               For fair without the fair within to hide.   90
               That book in many's eyes doth share the glory,
               That in gold clasps locks in the golden story;
               So shall you share all that he doth possess,
               By having him making yourself no less.

NURSE   No less? Nay, bigger! Women grow by men.   95

WIFE   Speak briefly, can you like of Paris' love?

JULIET   I'll look to like, if looking liking move;
               But no more deep will I endart mine eye
               Than your consent gives strength to make it fly.
               [Enter Servingman]

NURSE	An honor? Since I am your only nurse, I think you have gained wisdom from suckling at my breast.
WIFE	Give some thought to marriage. In Verona, younger girls than you are already mothers. I became your mother when I was your age. I will be brief: Paris wants to marry you.
NURSE	What a man, Juliet! Such a man in all the world—why, he is as fine as a wax statue.
WIFE	There's no finer man in Verona.
NURSE	Indeed, he is a choice husband—the flower of manhood.
WIFE	What is your answer? Can you love him? Tonight you will see him at dinner. Study his face and notice his handsome features, examine the harmony of his form, and see how balanced he is. What you don't see in his form, look for in his eyes. To complete this love match, this unattached male needs only marriage. As fish live in the sea, he is a beautiful creature swimming in a beautiful setting. Like a good book, he is handsome on the outside. Open the clasps and you find him handsome as well on the inside. You will share his property and still maintain your inheritance. You won't be any the less for marrying him.
NURSE	Make her less? She will grow bigger. Men make women grow bigger.
WIFE	Tell me, can you love Paris?
JULIET	I will expect to like him if what I see makes me like him, But I will go no farther than you approve. *[Enter Servingman]*

ACT I

SERVINGMAN   Madam, the guests are come, supper   100
served up, you called, my young lady asked for, the
nurse cursed in the pantry, and everything in extremity.
I must hence to wait. I beseech you follow straight.

WIFE   We follow thee. *[Exit Servingman]*
Juliet, the County stays.   105

NURSE   Go, girl, seek happy nights to happy days.
[Exeunt]

SERVINGMAN	Madam, the guests are here, supper is served, you and Juliet are summoned, the pantry servants curse the nurse, and everything's in a mess. I must go back to serve the guests. Please come soon.
WIFE	We will follow you. *[Servingman leaves]* Juliet, Count Paris is waiting.
NURSE	Go, child, look for happy nights for your happy days. *[They go out]*

ACT I, SCENE 4

The same. A street.

[Enter ROMEO, MERCUTIO, BENVOLIO, with five or six other Maskers; Torchbearers]

ROMEO	What, shall this speech be spoke for our excuse?
	Or shall we on without apology?
BENVOLIO	The date is out of such prolixity.
	We'll have no Cupid hoodwinked with a scarf,
	Bearing a Tartar's painted bow of lath,	5
	Scaring the ladies like a crowkeeper;
	Nor no without-book prologue, faintly spoke
	After the prompter, for our entrance;
	But, let them measure us by what they will,
	We'll measure them a measure and be gone.	10
ROMEO	Give me a torch. I am not for this ambling.
	Being but heavy, I will bear the light.
MERCUTIO	Nay, gentle Romeo, we must have you dance.
ROMEO	Not I, believe me. You have dancing shoes
	With nimble soles; I have a soul of lead	15
	So stakes me to the ground I cannot move.
MERCUTIO	You are a lover. Borrow Cupid's wings
	And soar with them above a common bound.
ROMEO	I am too sore enpierced with his shaft
	To soar with his light feathers; and so bound	20
	I cannot bound a pitch above dull woe.
	Under love's heavy burden do I sink.
MERCUTIO	And, to sink in it, should you burden love—
	Too great oppression for a tender thing.
ROMEO	Is love a tender thing? It is too rough,	25
	Too rude, too boist'rous, and it pricks like thorn.
MERCUTIO	If love be rough with you, be rough with love,
	Prick love for pricking, and you beat love down.
	Give me a case to put my visage in.
	A visor for a visor! What care I	30
	What curious eye doth quote deformities?
	Here are the beetle brows shall blush for me.

ORIGINAL

ACT I, SCENE 4

Again, a street in Verona.

[Entering are ROMEO, MERCUTIO, BENVOLIO, with five or six other youths wearing masks. Accompanying them are torchbearers to light the dark street]

ROMEO	How do we explain arriving at the dinner without invitations? Or shall we make no apology?
BENVOLIO	Such excuse-making is old-fashioned. We won't present a spokesman disguised as a masked Cupid and carrying a bow made out of a painted stick. He might alarm the ladies like a scarecrow. We won't make a memorized speech, whispered with prompts from the group, to explain our arrival. Let them size us up as they wish. We'll dance one dance and leave.
ROMEO	Hand me a torch. I hate dawdling along. Because I have a heavy heart, I will carry the light.
MERCUTIO	No, Romeo. We want you to dance, too.
ROMEO	Not me, I assure you. You have on dancing shoes with light soles. My soul is as heavy as lead. It weights me to the ground. I can't move.
MERCUTIO	You are in love. Borrow Cupid's wings and fly above earthly limits.
ROMEO	I am too sore from the wound made by his arrow to soar with light feathers at the dance. I am so bound up with emotion that I can't bound upwards above my aching heart. I sink from the heavy burden of romance.
MERCUTIO	You would be too heavy a load for Cupid if you would sink in love. A heavy heart oppresses a tender thing like infatuation.
ROMEO	Is love tender? To me it is harsh, rude, noisy, and prickly like a thorn.
MERCUTIO	If romance treats you harshly, then fight back. You can beat love if you give back what it gives you. Hand me a mask to hide my face. A mask for a masker! What do I care if someone stares at my face to remember its features. My own forehead shall do the blushing.

TRANSLATION

BENVOLIO	Come, knock and enter; and no sooner in But every man betake him to his legs.

ROMEO	A torch for me! Let wantons light of heart	35
	Tickle the senseless rushes with their heels;	
	For I am proverbed with a grandsire phrase,	
	I'll be a candle-holder and look on;	
	The game was ne'er so fair, and I am done.	

MERCUTIO	Tut! dun's the mouse, the constable's own word!	40
	If thou art Dun, we'll draw thee from the mire	
	Of this sir-reverence love, within thou stickest	
	Up to the ears. Come, we burn daylight, ho!	

ROMEO	Nay, that's not so.	
MERCUTIO	I mean, sir, in delay	
	We waste our lights in vain, like lamps by day.	45
	Take our good meaning, for our judgment sits	
	Five times in that ere once in our five wits.	
ROMEO	And we mean well in going to this masque,	
	But 'tis no wit to go.	
MERCUTIO	Why, may one ask?	
ROMEO	I dreamt a dream to-night.	
MERCUTIO	And so did I.	50
ROMEO	Well, what was yours?	
MERCUTIO	That dreamers often lie.	
ROMEO	In bed asleep, while they do dream things true.	

MERCUTIO	O, then I see Queen Mab hath been with you.	
	She is the fairies' midwife, and she comes	
	In shape no bigger than an agate stone	55
	On the forefinger of an alderman,	
	Drawn with a team of little atomies	
	Over men's noses as they lie asleep;	
	Her wagon spokes made of long spinners' legs,	
	The cover, of the wings of grasshoppers;	60
	Her traces, of the smallest spider web;	
	Her collars, of the moonshine's wat'ry beams;	
	Her whip, of cricket's bone; the lash, of film;	
	Her wagoner, a small grey-coated gnat,	
	Not half so big as a round little worm	65
	Pricked from the lazy finger of a maid;	

BENVOLIO	Let's knock at the door. As soon as we enter, everybody dance.
ROMEO	Hand me a torch! Let party-goers dance over the herb-strewn floor. As the saying goes, I will hold the candle and be the onlooker. Frolicking is not much fun. I am finished with it.
MERCUTIO	Hush. Fade into the company like a brown mouse and be quiet, as the sheriff warns. If you are dark-colored, we'll pull you out of the—pardon me—muck of your romance, where you are mired up to your ears. Come on. We're wasting time.
ROMEO	No, you're wrong.
MERCUTIO	I mean that, by dallying in the street, we waste our lives, like burning lamps in daytime. Understand me, for I speak for five party-goers, who make up five opinions.
ROMEO	We mean no harm in going to the party. It is no great thing to attend.
MERCUTIO	Why do you say that?
ROMEO	I had a dream last night.
MERCUTIO	Me too.
ROMEO	What was your dream?
MERCUTIO	That dreamers often lie.
ROMEO	Yes—they lie in bed and dream the truth.
MERCUTIO	I see that the fairy queen has visited you. She is midwife to the fairies. She is no taller than the stone in the ring on a city councilman's finger. Pulling her along are a team of tiny creatures that travel across men's noses while they sleep. The spokes of her wheels are made from spiders' legs. Covering her wagon are grasshoppers' wings. Her harness is the web of the smallest spider. Her horse collars are made from moonbeams. Her whip is a cricket's bone; the lashing end of her whip is a filmy thread. Her wagoneer is a gray gnat, half of the size of an earthworm plucked from a girl's finger.

Her chariot is an empty hazelnut,
Made by the joiner squirrel or old grub,
Time out o' mind the fairies' coachmakers.
And in this state she gallops by night   70
Through lovers' brains, and then they dream of love;
O'er courtiers' knees, that dream on curtsies straight;
O'er lawyers' fingers, who straight dream on fees;
O'er ladies' lips, who straight on kisses dream,
Which oft the angry Mab with blisters plagues,   75
Because their breaths with sweetmeats tainted are
Sometimes she gallops o'er a courtier's nose,
And then dreams he of smelling out a suit;
And sometime comes she with a tithe-pig's tail
Tickling a parson's nose as 'a lies asleep,   80
Then dreams he of another benefice.
Sometimes she driveth o'er a soldier's neck,
And then dreams he of cutting foreign throats,
Of breaches, ambuscadoes, Spanish blades,
Of healths five fathom deep; and then anon   85
Drums in his ear, at which he starts and wakes,
And being thus frighted, swears a prayer or two
And sleeps again. This is that very Mab
That plats the manes of horses in the night
And bakes the elflocks in foul sluttish hairs,   90
Which once untangled much misfortune bodes.
This is the hag, when maids lie on their backs,
That presses them and learns them first to bear,
Making them women of good carriage.
This is she—

ROMEO   Peace, peace, Mercutio, peace!   95
Thou talk'st of nothing.

MERCUTIO   True, I talk of dreams;
Which are the children of an idle brain,
Begot of nothing but vain fantasy;
Which is as thin of substance as the air,
And more inconstant than the wind, who woos   100
Even now the frozen bosom of the North
And, being angered, puffs away from thence,
Turning his side to the dew-dropping South.

Her chariot is a hazelnut shell built by a squirrel carpenter or by a grub worm, the traditional coach builder for the fairies. In her coach, she gallops through lovers' heads each night and brings them romantic dreams. She crosses the knees of courtiers, who see themselves in dreams making proper gestures to royalty. She crosses the fingers of attorneys, who dream of the money they will earn. She crosses ladies' lips, making them dream of kisses. When she's angry she gives those lips blisters. Because the ladies' breath is heavy with stale snacks, the fairy queen sometimes gallops over the courtier's nose, making him dream of sniffing out a chance for promotion. Sometimes she carries the tail of a pig delivered to a church as an offering. The tail tickles the preacher's nose as he lies asleep, making him dream of another church job. Sometimes she drives over a soldier's neck. Then he dreams of cutting the enemies' throats, of gaps in the enemy line, of ambushes, of Spanish swords, and of making a toast to health in wine thirty feet deep. In an instant, he hears military drums. Startled, he wakes up in fear, swears his faith in God a few times, then falls asleep again. This is the same fairy queen who tangles horses' manes in the night and snarls dirty hair that hurts the head when it's combed out. This is the evil woman who encourages young girls to lie on their backs, then they learn about sex and childbirth. This is the fairy—

ROMEO Hush, Mercutio, hush! You are talking nonsense.

MERCUTIO True. I am describing dreams. They are the offspring of an idle mind, formed of nothing but imaginings. Dreams are as empty as air, less predictable than the wind, which blows first to the North Pole, then, in a huff, it shifts to the dewy South.

TRANSLATION

| BENVOLIO | This wind you talk of blows us from ourselves. |
| | Supper is done, and we shall come too late. |

105

ROMEO	I fear, too early; for my mind misgives
	Some consequence, yet hanging in the stars,
	Shall bitterly begin his fearful date
	With this night's revels and expire the term
	Of a despised life, closed in my breast,
	By some vile forfeit of untimely death.
	But he that hath the steerage of my course
	Direct my sail! On, lusty gentlemen!

110

| BENVOLIO | Strike, drum. |

BENVOLIO   Your windy talk blows us away from our purpose. Dinner is over. We will arrive too late.

ROMEO   I'm afraid we will be too early. I sense some fearful encounter ordained by the heavens that will begin tonight. The event will end my life at a young age. But whatever the outcome, sail on, gentlemen!

BENVOLIO   Beat the drum.

ACT I, SCENE 5

The same. A hall in Capulet's house.

[They march about the stage, and Servingmen come forth with napkins]

1ST SERVINGMAN	Where's Potpan, that he helps not to take away? He shift a trencher? he scrape a trencher!
2ND SERVINGMAN	When good manners shall lie all in one or two men's hands, and they unwashed too, 'tis a foul thing. 5
1ST SERVINGMAN	Away with the joint-stools, remove the court-cupboard, look to the plate. Good thou, save me a piece of marchpane and, as thou loves me, let the porter let in Susan Grindstone and Nell. *[Exit second Servingman]* Anthony, and Potpan! 10 *[Enter two more Servingmen]*
3RD SERVINGMAN	Ay, boy, ready.
1ST SERVINGMAN	You are looked for and called for, asked for and sought for, in the great chamber.
4TH SERVINGMAN	We cannot be here and there too. Cheerly, boys! Be brisk awhile, and the longer liver take all. 15 *[Exit third and fourth Servingmen. Enter CAPULET, his WIFE, JULIET, TYBALT, NURSE, and all the Guests and Gentlewomen to the Maskers]*
CAPULET	Welcome, gentlemen! Ladies that have their toes Unplagued with corns will walk a bout with you. Ah ha, my mistresses! which of you all Will now deny to dance? She that makes dainty, She I'll swear hath corns. Am I come near ye now? 20 Welcome, gentlemen! I have seen the day That I have worn a visor and could tell A whispering tale in a fair lady's ear, Such as would please. 'Tis gone, 'tis gone, 'tis gone! You are welcome, gentlemen! Come, musicians, play. 25 *[Music plays, and they dance]* A hall, a hall! give room! and foot it, girls. More light, you knaves! and turn the tables up, And quench the fire, the room is grown too hot. Ah, sirrah, this unlooked-for sport comes well.

ORIGINAL

ACT I, SCENE 5

Again, a hall in Capulet's house.

[ROMEO, MERCUTIO, and the other maskers march on to the beat of the drummer. At the Capulet house, servants distribute napkins to the guests as they finish dinner]

1ST SERVINGMAN	Where's Potpan? He's supposed to clear the tables. Is he moving a plate or scraping dirty dishes?
2ND SERVINGMAN	It's disgusting that all the courtesies to diners are the work of one or two men, who serve guests without washing their hands.
1ST SERVINGMAN	Fold up the stools, remove the serving cart, take special care of the silverware. Friend, save me a bite of marzipan candy. Have the gatekeeper admit Susan Grindstone and Nell. *[Second Servingman leaves]* Anthony and Potpan! *[Two more servants enter]*
3RD SERVINGMAN	I'm ready.
1ST SERVINGMAN	We were looking for you and calling you. We asked about you in the main hall.
4TH SERVINGMAN	We can't be in the kitchen and, at the same time, in the great hall. Heartily, boys! Stay on your toes. The one who outlives the rest will win all. *[The third and fourth servants leave. Entering are CAPULET, his WIFE, JULIET, TYBALT, NURSE, and the guests to greet the masked men at the entrance]*
CAPULET	Welcome, gentlemen! The ladies who have no corns on their toes will dance with you. Well, my ladies, which of you will refuse to dance? The shy ones, who will pretend to have corns. Have I hurt your feelings, ladies? Welcome, gentlemen! I once put on a mask and whispered sweet nothings into a lady's ear. Those days are gone, gone, gone! You are welcome, gentlemen! Musicians, play music. *[Music plays, and they dance]* Make room! Dance well, girls. Servants, more light and fold up the tables. Put out the hearth fire. This hall is too warm. Ah, gentleman, this unexpected visit is a treat.

Nay, sit, nay, sit, good cousin Capulet,   30
For you and I are past our dancing days.
How long is't now since last yourself and I
Were in a mask?

2ND CAPULET   By'r Lady, thirty years.

CAPULET   What, man? 'Tis not so much, 'tis not so much;
'Tis since the nuptial of Lucentio,   35
Come Pentecost as quickly as it will,
Some five-and-twenty years, and then we masked.

2ND CAPULET   'Tis more, 'tis more. His son is elder, sir;
His son is thirty.

CAPULET   Will you tell me that?
His son was but a ward two years ago.   40

ROMEO   *[To a Servingman]* What lady's that, which doth enrich
the hand
Of yonder knight?

SERVINGMAN   I know not, sir.

ROMEO   O, she doth teach the torches to burn bright!
It seems she hangs upon the cheek of night   45
As a rich jewel in an Ethiop's ear—
Beauty too rich for use, for earth too dear!
So shows a snowy dove trooping with crows
As yonder lady o'er her fellows shows.
The measure done, I'll watch her place of stand   50
And, touching hers, make blessed my rude hand.
Did my heart love till now? Forswear it, sight!
For I ne'er saw true beauty till this night.

TYBALT   This, by his voice, should be a Montague.
Fetch me my rapier, boy. What, dares the slave   55
Come hither, covered with an antic face,
To fleer and scorn at our solemnity?
Now, by the stock and honor of my kin,
To strike him dead I hold it not a sin.

CAPULET   Why, how now, kinsman? Wherefore storm you so?   60

TYBALT   Uncle, this is a Montague, our foe;
A villain, that is thither come in spite
To scorn at our solemnity this night.

ORIGINAL

Sit, please, cousin Capulet. You and I are too old for dancing. How long has it been since we wore masks?

2ND CAPULET By the Virgin Mary, it's been thirty years.

CAPULET What? It hasn't been that long. It was at Lucentio's wedding. After Easter, it will be twenty-five years since we wore masks.

2ND CAPULET It has to be longer than that. Lucentio's son is thirty years old.

CAPULET You can't mean it! His son was a only a boy two years ago.

ROMEO *[To a servant]* Who is that lady, the one who adorns the hand of that man?

SERVINGMAN I don't know, sir.

ROMEO O, she outshines the torches! She bejewels the night like an earring in an African's ear—she is too beautiful for the ordinary woman, too precious to be mortal. Compared to the other women, she is a dove among crows. When this dance ends, I'll stand close to her and touch her hand with mine. Have I ever been in love before? Give it up, my eyes! I have never seen real beauty until tonight.

TYBALT By his voice, I recognize a Montague. Boy, bring me my sword. How dare you come in a mask to mock our gathering? Out of family honor, I think it won't be a sin to kill him dead.

CAPULET What are you doing, kinsman? Why all the noise?

TYBALT Uncle, this man is a Montague, our enemy. He is a villain come to mock this night's gathering.

CAPULET	Young Romeo is it?	
TYBALT	'Tis he, that villain Romeo.	
CAPULET	Content thee, gentle coz, let him alone.	65
	'A bears him like a portly gentleman,	
	And, to say truth, Verona brags of him	
	To be a virtuous and well-governed youth.	
	I would not for the wealth of all this town	
	Here in my house do him disparagement.	70
	Therefore be patient, take no note of him.	
	It is my will, the which if thou respect,	
	Show a fair presence and put off these frowns.	
	An ill-beseeming semblance for a feast.	
TYBALT	It fits when such a villain is a guest.	75
	I'll not endure him.	
CAPULET	He shall be endured.	
	What, goodman boy! I say he shall. Go to!	
	Am I the master here, or you? Go to!	
	You'll not endure him, God shall mend my soul!	
	You'll make a mutiny among my guests!	80
	You will set cock-a-hoop, you'll be the man!	
TYBALT	Why, uncle, 'tis a shame.	
CAPULET	Go to, go to!	
	You are a saucy boy. Is't so, indeed?	
	This trick may chance to scathe you, I know what.	
	You must contrary me! Marry, 'tis time—	85
	Well said, my hearts!—You are a princox—go!	
	Be quiet, or—More light, more light!—For shame!	
	I'll make you quiet; what!—Cheerly, my hearts!	
TYBALT	Patience perforce with willful choler meeting	
	Makes my flesh tremble in their different greeting.	90
	I will withdraw; but this intrusion shall,	
	Now seeming sweet, convert to bitt'rest gall.	
	[Exit]	
ROMEO	If I profane with my unworthiest hand	
	This holy shrine, the gentle sin is this;	
	My lips, two blushing pilgrims, ready stand	95
	To smooth that rough touch with a tender kiss.	

ORIGINAL

CAPULET	Is it young Romeo?
TYBALT	It is, that despicable Romeo.
CAPULET	Calm down, cousin, let him be. He behaves well. The people of Verona call him a young gentleman, honorable and dignified. I wouldn't for all the money in Verona insult him in my home. Be calm and ignore him. I insist that you respect my wishes. Be polite and stop scowling. Your behavior is out of place at a feast.
TYBALT	My behavior suits so dishonorable a guest. I won't tolerate him.
CAPULET	You will tolerate him. You young sprout! I say that he is welcome. Behave yourself! I am the host, not you! You have the nerve to insult him? God help me if I allow it! You want a ruckus among the guests? You want a free-for-all? You want to be the host?
TYBALT	Uncle, this guest shames you.
CAPULET	Hush. You are impertinent. Is Romeo shaming me? Your hostility may injure you, of that I am sure. You want to disobey me! I suppose you're at the age to rebel—*[to the guests]* Good joke, my friends!—*[to TYBALT]* You are the prince of peacocks—out with you! Hush or—bring more light!—Shame on you! I'll make you hush!—*[to the guests]* Have a good time!
TYBALT	I can't stand anger and tolerance all at the same time. I will leave the room. But Romeo's intrusion, which seems pleasant now, will change into bitter enmity. *[He leaves]*
ROMEO	If I dirty with my unworthy hand this sacred flesh, I will pay a fine. My blushing lips, like holy pilgrims, are ready to brush away that rough touch with a gentle kiss.

JULIET	Good pilgrim, you do wrong your hand too much,
	Which mannerly devotion shows in this;
	For saints have hands that pilgrims' hands do touch,
	And palm to palm is holy palmers' kiss.	100

ROMEO   Have not saints lips, and holy palmers too?

JULIET   Ay, pilgrim, lips that they must use in prayer.

ROMEO   O, then, dear saint, let lips do what hands do!
They pray; grant thou, lest faith turn to despair.

JULIET   Saints do not move, though grant for prayers' sake.   105

ROMEO   Then move not while my prayer's effect I take.
Thus from my lips, by thine my sin is purged.
[Kisses her]

JULIET   Then have my lips the sin that they have took.

ROMEO   Sin from my lips? O trespass sweetly urged!
Give me my sin again *[Kisses her]*

JULIET   You kiss by th' book.   110

NURSE   Madam, your mother craves a word with you.

ROMEO   What is her mother?

NURSE   Marry, bachelor,
Her mother is the lady of the house,
And a good lady, and a wise and virtuous.
I nursed her daughter that you talked withal.   115
I tell you, he that can lay hold of her
Shall have the chinks.

ROMEO   Is she a Capulet?
O dear account! my life is my foe's debt.

BENVOLIO   Away, be gone; the sport is at the best.

ROMEO   Ay, so I fear; the more is my unrest.   120

CAPULET   Nay, gentlemen, prepare not to be gone;
We have a trifling foolish banquet towards.
Is it e'en so? Why then, I thank you all.
I thank you, honest gentlemen. Good night.
More torches here! Come on then, let's to bed.   125
Ah, sirrah, by my fay, it waxes late;
I'll to my rest.
[Exeunt all but JULIET and NURSE]

ORIGINAL

JULIET	Good pilgrim, you accuse your hand wrongly. You express polite devotion by touching me. Even saints let religious pilgrims kiss their hands. And holy palm-bearers touch hand to hand.
ROMEO	Don't saints and palm-bearers have ordinary lips?
JULIET	Yes, pilgrim, but they use their lips to pray.
ROMEO	Dear saintly girl, let's touch lips the same way that we touch hands! Lips convey prayers to keep faith from turning into despair.
JULIET	Saints do not change their behavior just for the sake of human prayers.
ROMEO	Then stand still while I kiss you. By touching your saintly lips, mine are forgiven of their sin. *[Kisses her]*
JULIET	Then let my lips accept your sin.
ROMEO	Do my lips commit a sin? Oh sweet fault sweetly requested! Let me sin again. *[Kisses her]*
JULIET	You kiss like someone who has studied romance.
NURSE	Madam, your mother wants to talk to you.
ROMEO	Who is her mother?
NURSE	Indeed, young man, her mother is mistress of the Capulet household. She is a good lady, both wise and respectable. I was wetnurse to Juliet, to whom you were speaking. I promise you, the man that marries her will receive a large dowry.
ROMEO	Is she a Capulet? Oh terrible news, I must give my life to an enemy.
BENVOLIO	Let's go. We've had our fun.
ROMEO	I suspect that our good time will trouble me.
CAPULET	No, gentlemen, don't go. We will have a light banquet after the dance. Must you go? Well, I thank you all. My thanks, gentlemen. Good night. Bring more light to the door. Let's go to bed. It's late. I need my rest. *[All but JULIET and her NURSE go out]*

JULIET	Come hither, Nurse. What is yond gentleman?
NURSE	The son and heir of old Tiberio.
JULIET	What's he that now is going out of door?

130

NURSE	Marry, that, I think, be young Petruchio.
JULIET	What's he that follows there, that would not dance?
NURSE	I know not.
JULIET	Go ask his name.—If he be married,
	My grave is like to be my wedding bed.

135

NURSE	His name is Romeo, and a Montague,
	The only son of your great enemy.
JULIET	My only love, sprung from my only hate!
	Too early seen unknown, and known too late!
	Prodigious birth of love it is to me

140

	That I must love a loathed enemy.
NURSE	What's this? what's this?
JULIET	A rhyme I learnt even now
	Of one I danced withal. *[One calls within, 'Juliet']*
NURSE	Anon, anon!
	Come, let's away; the strangers all are gone.
	[Exeunt]

JULIET	Come here, nurse. Who is that man there?
NURSE	Old Tiberio's son and heir.
JULIET	Who is that going out the door?
NURSE	I think that he is young Petruchio.
JULIET	Who is the man that follows Petruchio, the guest who would not dance?
NURSE	I don't know.
JULIET	Find out his name. If he is married, I will die a virgin.
NURSE	He is Romeo of the Montague family. He is the only son of your family's great enemy.
JULIET	My only love is the son of my only enemy! I didn't know him at first. Now it's too late to stop loving him! This romance is ominous. I am in love with my family's foe.
NURSE	What? What are you saying?
JULIET	A jingle that I learned from one of my dance partners. *[Someone calls "Juliet"]*
NURSE	Hurry up! Let's go. The guests have all gone home. *[They depart]*

TRANSLATION

ACT II, PROLOGUE

[Enter Chorus]

CHORUS
Now old desire doth in his deathbed lie,
   And young affection gapes to be his heir;
That fair for which love groaned for and would die,
   With tender Juliet matched, is now not fair.
Now Romeo is beloved and loves again,   5
   Alike bewitched by the charm of looks;
But to his foe supposed he must complain,
   And she steal love's sweet bait from fearful hooks.
Being held a foe, he may not have access
   To breathe such vows as lovers use to swear,   10
And she as much in love, her means much less
   To meet her new beloved anywhere;
But passion lends them power, time means, to meet,
   Temp'ring extremities with extreme sweet. *[Exeunt]*

ACT II, PROLOGUE

[The narrator enters]

CHORUS   As an old romance ends, a young love pushes into the
heart. The girl for whom Romeo pined has given place
to Juliet. This time, Romeo both loves and is beloved.
Enchanting both boy and girl are mutual looks of love.
But he must profess his love to an assumed enemy and
she must snatch the bait from a deadly hook. Because he
is an enemy, he has no access to the girl whom he wants
to court. Although she loves him in return, she has no
opportunity to be alone with him. Passion empowers
them to meet by overcoming obstacles with sweet trickery.
[The narrator departs]

ACT II

ACT II, SCENE 1

Verona. A lane by the wall of Capulet's orchard.

[Enter ROMEO alone]

ROMEO   Can I go forward when my heart is here?
              Turn back, dull earth, and find thy centre out.
              [Enter BENVOLIO with MERCUTIO. ROMEO retires]

BENVOLIO   Romeo! My cousin Romeo! Romeo!

MERCUTIO   He is wise,
              And, on my life, hath stol'n him home to bed.

BENVOLIO   He ran this way and leapt this orchard wall.   5
              Call, good Mercutio.

MERCUTIO   Nay, I'll conjure too.
              Romeo! humors! madman! passion! lover!
              Appear thou in the likeness of a sigh!
              Speak but one rhyme, and I am satisfied!
              Cry but 'Ay me!' pronounce but 'love' and 'dove';   10
              Speak to my gossip Venus one fair word,
              One nickname for her purblind son and heir
              Young Abraham Cupid, he that shot so true
              When King Cophetua loved the beggar maid!
              He heareth not, he stirreth not, he moveth not;   15
              The ape is dead, and I must conjure him.
              I conjure thee by Rosaline's bright eyes,
              By her high forehead and her scarlet lip,
              By her fine foot, straight leg, and quivering thigh,
              And the demesnes that there adjacent lie,   20
              That in thy likeness thou appear to us!

BENVOLIO   An if he hear thee, thou wilt anger him.

MERCUTIO   This cannot anger him, 'Twould anger him
              To raise a spirit in his mistress' circle
              Of some strange nature, letting it there stand   25
              Till she had laid it and conjured it down.
              That were some spite; my invocation
              Is fair and honest: in his mistress' name,
              I conjure only but to raise up him.

BENVOLIO   Come, he hath hid himself among these trees   30
              To be consorted with the humorous night.
              Blind is his love and best befits the dark.

ORIGINAL

ACT II, SCENE 1

Verona. A lane by the wall of Capulet's orchard.

[Enter ROMEO alone]

ACT II

ROMEO   Can I go on my way when my heart belongs here with Juliet? Turn back, dullard, and find your core with Juliet. *[BENVOLIO enters with MERCUTIO. ROMEO withdraws]*

BENVOLIO   Romeo! My cousin, Romeo!

MERCUTIO   He is smart in returning home to bed.

BENVOLIO   He ran down this lane and jumped over this orchard wall. Call him, Mercutio.

MERCUTIO   I'll lure him. Romeo! Moody madman! Passionate lover! Speak one verse and I will be satisfied! Call out, "Ah, me!" Say "love" and "dove." Speak one word to my confidante Venus, the goddess of passion. Give one nickname to her blind son Cupid, he who shot an arrow into King Cophetua that made him fall for the beggar girl Penelophon! Romeo hears nothing. He doesn't stir or rise. The poor soul is dead. I must enchant him. I charm you, Romeo, by Rosaline's bright eyes, high forehead, scarlet lips, dainty feet, straight legs, and quivering thighs. I charm you by the territory that lies between her thighs that you appear to us in the flesh!

BENVOLIO   If he hears you, he is going to be mad.

MERCUTIO   I didn't anger him. He would be mad if I summoned a supernatural spirit in his lover's genitals and let it stay until she grasped it and charmed it back down. That would arouse hostility. My call is not harmful. I charm him by his lover's name only to uplift him.

BENVOLIO   Let's go. He is hidden in these trees to wait for night. His love is blind, well suited to the dark.

TRANSLATION

MERCUTIO	If love be blind, love cannot hit the mark.
	Now will he sit under a medlar tree
	And wish his mistress were that kind of fruit	35
	As maids call medlars when they laugh alone.
	O, Romeo, that she were, O that she were
	An open et cetera and thou a pop'rin pear!
	Romeo, good night. I'll to my truckle-bed;
	This field-bed is too cold for me to sleep.	40
	Come shall we go?

BENVOLIO   Go then, for 'tis in vain
To seek him here that means not to be found.
[Exit with MERCUTIO]

MERCUTIO   If love is blind, then Cupid can't hit the target with his arrow. Now he will sit under a medlar tree and wish his lover were the kind of apple that girls call "meddlers" when there is no one to hear them. Oh, Romeo, if she were only an open unmentionable and you were a Belgian pear! Romeo, good night. I'm off to my little bed. Sleeping in the field is too cold for me. Shall we go, Benvolio?

BENVOLIO   Let's go. It is useless to look for him here when he doesn't want to be found. *[He departs with MERCUTIO]*

ACT II

ACT II, SCENE 2

The same. Capulet's orchard.

ROMEO   *[Coming forward]*
He jests at scars that never felt a wound.
[Enter JULIET above at a window]
But soft! What light through yonder window breaks?
It is the East, and Juliet is the sun!
Arise, fair sun, and kill the envious moon,
Who is already sick and pale with grief   5
That thou her maid art far more fair than she.
Be not her maid, since she is envious.
Her vestal livery is but sick and green,
And none but fools do wear it. Cast it off.
It is my lady; O, it is my love!   10
O that she knew she were!
She speaks, yet she says nothing. What of that?
Her eye discourses; I will answer it.
I am too bold; 'tis not to me she speaks.
Two of the fairest stars in all the heaven,   15
Having some business, do entreat her eyes
To twinkle in their spheres till they return.
What if her eyes were there, they in her head?
The brightness of her cheek would shame those stars
As daylight doth a lamp; her eyes in heaven   20
Would through the airy region stream so bright
That birds would sing and think it were not night.
See how she leans her cheek upon her hand!
O that I were a glove upon that hand,
That I might touch that cheek!

JULIET   Ay me!

ROMEO   She speaks.   25
O speak again, bright angel! for thou art
As glorious to this night, being o'er my head,
As is a winged messenger of heaven
Unto the white-upturned wond'ring eyes
Of mortals that fall back to gaze on him   30
When he bestrides the lazy-pacing clouds
And sails upon the bosom of the air.

JULIET   O Romeo, Romeo! wherefore art thou Romeo?
Deny thy father and refuse thy name;
Or, if thou wilt not, be but sworn my love,   35
And I'll no longer be a Capulet.

ORIGINAL

ACT II, SCENE 2

The same. Capulet's orchard.

ROMEO *[Coming forward]* Mercutio ridicules lovers' scars when he has never been shot by Cupid's arrow. *[Enter JULIET above at a window]* But quiet! What is that light in the upper window? It is the east, and Juliet is the rising sun! Awaken, lovely sunrise, and outshine the envious moon, which turns pale because you are prettier than she. Don't be her lover, since she envies you. The moon's nun's habit is sickly and anemic. Only fools wear it. Throw it away. It is Juliet; Oh, it is my love! I wish she knew that I love her. She is speaking, but not saying anything. What does that mean? She looks around. I will talk to her. I am too daring. She isn't addressing me. While two bright stars in the skies depart on an errand, they ask her eyes to twinkle in their place. What if her eyes were in the sky rather than in her face? The glow of her cheek would shame those stars as much as daylight outshines a lamp. Her eyes in the sky would shine so brightly that birds would sing as though it were daytime. Look how she leans her cheek on her hand! I would love to be a glove on her hand and caress her cheek!

JULIET Oh me!

ROMEO She speaks. Oh say something else, bright angel! You are as glorious to the night sky as a winged angel from heaven. He pleases upturned human eyes that gaze back on him when he stands on clouds and sails in the air.

JULIET Oh Romeo, Romeo! Where are you, Romeo? Give up your father and your family name. If you refuse, then be my love and I will no longer be a Capulet.

TRANSLATION

ACT II

ROMEO	*[Aside]* Shall I hear more, or shall I speak at this?
JULIET	'Tis but thy name that is my enemy. Thou art thyself, though not a Montague. What's Montague? It is nor hand, nor foot, 40 Nor arm, nor face, nor any other part Belonging to a man. O, be some other name! What's in a name? That which we call a rose By any other word would smell as sweet. So Romeo would, were he not Romeo called, 45 Retain that dear perfection which he owcs Without that title. Romeo, doff thy name; And for thy name, which is no part of thee, Take all myself.
ROMEO	I take thee at thy word. Call me but love, and I'll be new baptized; 50 Henceforth I never will be Romeo.
JULIET	What man art thou that, thus bescreened in night, So stumblest on my counsel?
ROMEO	By a name I know not how to tell thee who I am. My name, dear saint, is hateful to myself, 55 Because it is an enemy to thee. Had I it written, I would tear the word.
JULIET	My ears have yet not drunk a hundred words Of thy tongue's uttering, yet I know the sound. Art thou not Romeo, and a Montague? 60
ROMEO	Neither, fair maid, if either thee dislike.
JULIET	How camest thou hither, tell me, and wherefore? The orchard walls are high and hard to climb, And the place death, considering who thou art, If any of my kinsmen find thee here. 65
ROMEO	With love's light wings did I o'erperch these walls; For stony limits cannot hold love out, And what love can do, that dares love attempt. Therefore thy kinsmen are no stop to me.
JULIET	If they do see thee, they will murder thee. 70
ROMEO	Alack, there lies more peril in thine eye Than twenty of their swords! Look thou but sweet, And I am proof against their enmity.
JULIET	I would not for the world they saw thee here.

ORIGINAL

ROMEO	*[To himself]* Shall I listen to more of her words, or shall I answer her?
JULIET	Only your name is hostile to me. You are you. Your surname means nothing. What is "Montague"? It isn't real flesh, like a hand, foot, arm, or face. Oh choose some other name! Why is the name important? What we call a "rose" would be still be fragrant if we gave it some other name. So Romeo would be as perfect if he were not called "Romeo." Romeo, drop your name. In place of a name, which is no physical part of you, take all of me.
ROMEO	I will do exactly what you say. Call me your lover and I will be christened again. From now on, I will not be called "Romeo."
JULIET	Who is out there in the dark, eavesdropping on my words?
ROMEO	I don't know how to identify myself by name. Dear saint, my name is disgusting to you because Capulets hate Montagues. If my name were on paper, I would tear it up.
JULIET	I have heard fewer than a hundred of your words, but I know your voice. Are you Romeo, a Montague?
ROMEO	I am neither, sweet girl, if you dislike those words.
JULIET	How and why do you come here? The orchard walls are tall and hard to climb. The place is deadly if my relatives find a Montague here.
ROMEO	With the wings of love, I hopped over these walls; for stone walls can't shut out romance. Love dares to try anything. Your relatives can't stop me.
JULIET	If they see you, they will murder you.
ROMEO	There is more risk in your eye than in twenty Capulet swords. Look sweetly down on me and I can prove my courage against my enemies.
JULIET	I wouldn't for anything have them find you here.

ACT II

TRANSLATION

ROMEO	I have night's cloak to hide me from their eyes;	75
	And but thou love me, let them find me here.	
	My life were better ended by their hate	
	Than death prorogued, wanting of thy love.	
JULIET	By whose direction found'st thou out this place?	
ROMEO	By love, that first did prompt me to inquire.	80
	He lent me counsel, and I lent him eyes.	
	I am no pilot; yet, wert thou as far	
	As that vast shore washed with the farthest sea,	
	I should adventure for such merchandise.	
JULIET	Thou knowest the mask of night is on my face;	85
	Else would a maiden blush bepaint my cheek	
	For that which thou hast heard me speak to-night.	
	Fain would I dwell on form—fain, fain deny	
	What I have spoke; but farewell compliment!	
	Dost thou love me? I know thou wilt say 'Ay';	90
	And I will take thy word. Yet, if thou swear'st,	
	Thou mayst prove false. At lovers' perjuries,	
	They say Jove laughs. O gentle Romeo,	
	If thou dost love, pronounce it faithfully.	
	Or if thou thinkest I am too quickly won,	95
	I'll frown, and be perverse, and say thee nay,	
	So thou wilt woo; but else, not for the world.	
	In truth, fair Montague, I am too fond,	
	And therefore thou mayst think my 'haviour light:	
	But trust me, gentleman, I'll prove more true	100
	Than those that have more cunning to be strange.	
	I should have been more strange, I must confess,	
	But that thou overheard'st, ere I was ware,	
	My true-love passion. Therefore pardon me,	
	And not impute this yielding to light love,	105
	Which the dark night hath so discovered.	
ROMEO	Lady, by yonder blessed moon I vow,	
	That tips with silver all these fruit-tree tops—	
JULIET	O, swear not by the moon, th' inconstant moon,	
	That monthly changes in her circled orb,	110
	Lest that thy love prove likewise variable.	
ROMEO	What shall I swear by?	
JULIET	Do not swear at all;	
	Or if thou wilt, swear by thy gracious self,	
	Which is the god of my idolatry,	
	And I'll believe thee.	

ORIGINAL

ROMEO	I have darkness to hide me. If you don't love me, then let them find me. I would rather die from their hatred than to die later for want of your love.
JULIET	Who showed you how to find this place?
ROMEO	Love caused me to ask. Love gave me advice; I used my eyes. I am no ship's pilot. But if you were washed up in a distant seashore, I would venture to the spot to claim you.
JULIET	You know that darkness conceals my face. Otherwise, I would blush for letting you overhear my words tonight. I would gladly be a proper young lady—I would gladly deny what you heard me say, but I abandon polite conversation. Do you love me? I know you will say "Yes" and I will accept your word. But if you confess your love, you may be lying. When lovers lie, they say that Jupiter laughs. Oh gentle Romeo, if you love me, tell me honestly. If you think I am too eager for your love, I will scowl and be difficult and say no to make you court me. If you don't think I am too quickly won, I wouldn't be difficult for all the world. I confess, handsome Montague, I am foolish and may cause you to think I am a silly girl. But trust me, sir. I will prove more faithful than craftier girls. I would have been more distant, I confess, but you have already overheard my true passion. Please pardon me. Don't accuse me of yielding too easily to love, which you have discovered from your hiding place in the dark.
ROMEO	Lady, I pledge by the moon, which brushes silver across the tops of fruit trees—
JULIET	Oh, don't pledge by the moon, the changeable moon, which makes an orbit each month, lest your love is similarly shifting.
ROMEO	What shall I pledge by?
JULIET	Don't swear at all. If you want to pledge, do so by your generous self, which I adore, and I will believe you.

ACT II

ROMEO   If my heart's dear love—   115

JULIET   Well, do not swear. Although I joy in thee,
                    I have no joy of this contract to-night.
                    It is too rash, too unadvised, too sudden;
                    Too like the lightning, which doth cease to be
                    Ere one can say 'It lightens.' Sweet, good night!   120
                    This bud of love, by summer's ripening breath,
                    May prove a beauteous flow'r when next we meet.
                    Good night, good night! As sweet repose and rest
                    Come to thy heart as that within my breast!

ROMEO   O, wilt thou leave me so unsatisfied?   125

JULIET   What satisfaction canst thou have to-night?

ROMEO   Th' exchange of thy love's faithful vow for mine.

JULIET   I gave thee mine before thou didst request it;
                    And yet I would it were to give again.

ROMEO   Wouldst thou withdraw it? For what purpose, love?   130

JULIET   But to be frank and give it thee again.
                    And yet I wish but for the thing I have.
                    My bounty is as boundless as the sea,
                    My love as deep; the more I give to thee,
                    The more I have, for both are infinite.   135
                    I hear some noise within. Dear love, adieu!
                    [Nurse calls within]
                    Anon, good nurse! Sweet Montague, be true.
                    Stay but a little, I will come again. *[Exit]*

ROMEO   O blessed, blessed night! I am afeard,
                    Being in night, all this is but a dream,   140
                    Too flattering-sweet to be substantial.
                    [Enter JULIET above]

JULIET   Three words, dear Romeo, and good night indeed.
                    If that thy bent of love be honorable,
                    Thy purpose marriage, send me word to-morrow,
                    By one that I'll procure to come to thee,   145
                    Where and what time thou wilt perform the rite;
                    And all my fortunes at thy foot I'll lay
                    And follow thee my lord throughout the world.

NURSE   *[Within]* Madam!

JULIET   I come, anon.—But if thou meanest not well,   150
                    I do beseech thee—

NURSE   *[Within]*
                    Madam!

ORIGINAL

ROMEO	If my heart's own beloved—
JULIET	Don't pledge. Although I delight in you, I don't rejoice in a pledge tonight. A promise is too hasty, too inadvisable, too soon, too much like lightning, which is gone before I can say "It is lightning." Sweet one, good night! This budding romance, by summer's ripening air, may turn into a beautiful blossom by the time that we next meet. Good night, good night! Let sweet rest come to your heart and to mine!
ROMEO	Will you leave me so unsatisfied?
JULIET	What satisfaction do you expect tonight?
ROMEO	Pledge your love to me.
JULIET	I gave you my love before you asked for it. If I still had it, I would give it to you again.
ROMEO	Would you take it back? Why, my love?
JULIET	To be sincere and give it to you again. I don't wish for more than your love. My generosity is deep like an ocean. The more love I give you, the more I have to give, for both the sea and my love are infinite. I hear a noise inside. Dear love, farewell! *[Nurse calls within] [To the nurse]* At once, sweet nurse! *[To Romeo]* Sweet Romeo, be faithful to me. Wait a bit and I will come back to the balcony. *[Juliet goes out]*
ROMEO	Oh blessed night! I fear that, because it is night, I am dreaming all this. Our conversation is too sweet, too dear to be real. *[Enter JULIET above]*
JULIET	Three more words, dear Romeo, and it is indeed a good night. If your intent is honorable and your goal is marriage, send me word tomorrow by the messenger I will send to you. Tell me where and what time you want the ceremony to take place. I will place before you all my hopes and follow you as my husband anywhere in the world.
NURSE	*[To Juliet]* Madam!
JULIET	*[To the nurse]* I am coming immediately. *[To Romeo]* But if you are lying, I beg you—
NURSE	*[To Juliet]* Madam!

ACT II

TRANSLATION

JULIET	By and by I come.—
	To cease thy suit and leave me to my grief.
	To-morrow will I send.
ROMEO	So thrive my soul—
JULIET	A thousand times good night! *[Exit]* 155
ROMEO	A thousand times the worse, to want thy light!
	Love goes toward love as schoolboys from their books;
	But love from love, toward school with heavy looks.
	[Enter JULIET, above, again]
JULIET	Hist! Romeo, hist! O for a falc'ner's voice
	To lure this tassel-gentle back again! 160
	Bondage is hoarse and may not speak aloud,
	Else would I tear the cave where Echo lies
	And make her airy tongue more hoarse than mine
	With repetition of 'My Romeo!'
ROMEO	It is my soul that calls upon my name. 165
	How silver-sweet sound lovers' tongues by night,
	Like softest music to attending ears!
JULIET	Romeo!
ROMEO	My sweet?
JULIET	At what o'clock to-morrow
	Shall I send to thee?
ROMEO	By the hour of nine.
JULIET	I will not fail. 'Tis twenty years till then. 170
	I have forgot why I did call thee back.
ROMEO	Let me stand here till thou remember it.
JULIET	I shall forget, to have thee still stand there,
	Rememb'ring how I love thy company.
ROMEO	And I'll still stay, to have thee still forget, 175
	Forgetting any other home but this.
JULIET	'Tis almost morning. I would have thee gone—
	And yet no farther than a wanton's bird,
	That lets it hop a little from her hand,
	Like a poor prisoner in his twisted gyves, 180
	And with a silken thread plucks it back again,
	So loving-jealous of his liberty.
ROMEO	I would I were thy bird.

ORIGINAL

JULIET	[To the nurse] I am coming at once. [To Romeo] Stop your courtship and leave me to pine for you. I will send a message tomorrow.
ROMEO	If I survive.
JULIET	A thousand good nights. [She departs]
ROMEO	A thousand times darker without your light! Love gravitates toward the beloved as schoolboys flee textbooks. When a lover leaves a beloved, it is like schoolboys frowning on their way to class. [Enter JULIET, above, again]
JULIET	Psst! Romeo, psst! I wish I had a falconer's voice to summon my sweet bird back again! Slavery is harsh and refuses free speech to the slave. Otherwise I would rip open Echo's cave and make her hoarse with cries of "My Romeo!"
ROMEO	She is my soul mate who calls my name. A lover's words sound silvery at night, like music to the ears of a music lover!
JULIET	Romeo!
ROMEO	Yes, my sweet?
JULIET	What time tomorrow shall I sent the messenger?
ROMEO	By 9:00 A.M.
JULIET	I won't fail. It will seem like twenty years until then. I have forgotten why I summoned you again.
ROMEO	I will stay here until you remember why.
JULIET	I will pretend to forget why to keep you standing there, recalling how much I love your company.
ROMEO	And I will keep on standing here to make you continue forgetting any other home but this.
JULIET	It is almost dawn. I would have you gone—but no further away than a pet bird from a girl who lets it hop from her hand. Like a little prisoner tied to a silk thread, I would pluck you back again because I resent your liberty to fly away.
ROMEO	I would like to be your pet bird.

ACT II

TRANSLATION

JULIET   Sweet, so would I.
                  Yet I should kill thee with much cherishing.
                  Good night, good night! Parting is such sweet sorrow   185
                  That I shall say good night till it be morrow. *[Exit]*

ROMEO   Sleep dwell upon thine eyes, peace in thy breast!
                  Would I were sleep and peace, so sweet to rest!
                  Hence will I to my ghostly father's cell,
                  His help to crave and my dear hap to tell. *[Exit]*   190

JULIET	Sweetheart, I wish you were my pet. But I might kill you from too much cherishing. Good night, good night! Parting is such a tender grief. I will say good night until tomorrow. *[She goes out]*
ROMEO	Sleep close your eyes; peace linger in your breast! I wish I were sleep and peace to rest so sweetly! I will go to my spiritual adviser's room and, after I tell him of my good fortune, beg his help. *[He goes out]*

TRANSLATION

ACT II, SCENE 3

The same. Friar Laurence's cell.

[Enter FRIAR LAURENCE alone, with a basket]

FRIAR   The grey-eyed morn smiles on the frowning night,
Check'ring the Eastern clouds with streaks of light;
And flecked darkness like a drunkard reels
From forth day's path and Titan's fiery wheels.
Now, ere the sun advance his burning eye   5
The day to cheer and night's dank dew to dry,
I must up-fill this osier cage of ours
With baleful weeds and precious-juiced flowers.
The earth that's nature's mother is her tomb.
What is her burying grave, that is her womb;   10
And from her womb children of divers kind
We sucking on her natural bosom find,
Many for many virtues excellent,
None but for some, and yet all different.
O, mickle is the powerful grace that lies   15
In plants, herbs, stones, and their true qualities;
For naught so vile that on the earth doth live
But to the earth some special good doth give;
Nor aught so good but, strained from that fair use,
Revolts from true birth, stumbling on abuse.   20
Virtue itself turns vice, being misapplied,
And vice sometime 's by action dignified.
[Enter ROMEO]
Within the infant rind of this weak flower
Poison hath residence, and medicine power;
For this, being smelt, with that part cheers each part;   25
Being tasted, slays all senses with the heart.
Two such opposed kings encamp them still
In man as well as herbs—grace and rude will;
And where the worser is predominant,
Full soon the canker death eats up that plant.   30

ROMEO   Good morrow, father.

ACT II, SCENE 3

The same night. Friar Laurence's room.

[Enter FRIAR LAURENCE alone, with a basket]

FRIAR   Gray morning lightens the dark of night, streaking eastern clouds with light. And spotted darkness like a drunkard totters out of the way of sunrise. Before morning lights up the sky and dries the dew, I must fill my basket with poisonous plants and succulent flowers. The earth is both parent and grave to nature. Nature is born on earth and is buried here. All earth's children emerge from her womb and take nourishment from nature. Much of earthly nourishment is excellent. All plants have some use. Each plant is different in its properties. Great is the generosity in plants, herbs, stones, and their inner value. Nothing on earth is so worthless that it doesn't give some good. And nothing is so good and so valuable that it can't be misused. Good things can become harmful if mis-used; similarly, evil sometimes can have a worthy purpose. *[Enter ROMEO]* Inside the seed husk of this weak flower is a substance that can be healing or poisonous. The flower, when sniffed, cheers with its fragrance; when swallowed, it stops the heart. Two similar opposites live in human beings. Just like herbs, they can be gracious or danger-ous, depending on the intent. When the evil power takes control, the plant dies of disease.

ROMEO   Good morning, father.

FRIAR	Benedicite!
	What early tongue so sweet saluteth me?
	Young son, it argues a distempered head
	So soon to bid good morrow to thy bed.
	Care keeps his watch in every old man's eye, 35
	And where care lodges, sleep will never lie;
	But where unbruised youth with unstuffed brain
	Doth couch his limbs, there golden sleep doth reign.
	Therefore thy earliness doth me assure
	Thou art uproused with some distemp'rature; 40
	Or if not so, then here I hit it right—
	Our Romeo hath not been in bed to-night.
ROMEO	That last is true—the sweeter rest was mine.
FRIAR	God pardon sin! Wast thou with Rosaline?
ROMEO	With Rosaline, my ghostly father? No. 45
	I have forgot that name and that name's woe.
FRIAR	That's my good son! But where hast thou been then?
ROMEO	I'll tell thee ere thou ask it me again.
	I have been feasting with mine enemy,
	Where on a sudden one hath wounded me 50
	That's by me wounded. Both our remedies
	Within thy help and holy physic lies.
	I bear no hatred, blessed man, for lo,
	My intercession likewise steads my foe.
FRIAR	Be plain, good son, and homely in thy drift. 55
	Riddling confession finds but riddling shrift.
ROMEO	Then plainly know my heart's dear love is set
	On the fair daughter of rich Capulet;
	As mine on hers, so hers is set on mine,
	And all combined, save what thou must combine 60
	By holy marriage. When, and where, and how
	We met, we wooed, and made exchange of vow,
	I'll tell thee as we pass; but this I pray,
	That thou consent to marry us to-day.

ORIGINAL

FRIAR	Bless you! What early riser is greeting me so sweetly? Son, only an uneasy mind would rouse you from bed so early. Worry keeps old men awake. Where there are troubles, sleep can't lie down. But untroubled youth can stretch out without worries and can sleep well. Your early arrival tells me that you haven't been able to rest. If you haven't slept, then I am right—Romeo didn't go to bed last night.

ROMEO	The last part is true—I enjoyed a sweeter kind of rest.
FRIAR	God pardon sin! Were you with Rosaline?
ROMEO	With Rosaline, my spiritual father? No. I have forgotten her name and the pain she brought me.
FRIAR	Good boy! But where were you last night?
ROMEO	I will tell you before you can ask a second time. I dined with my enemy. All at once, someone wounded me with a love dart and I did the same for her. The cure for both of us lies in your power and holy cure. I bear no ill will, dear man, for my request is beneficial to both me and my enemy.
FRIAR	Speak plainly, son, and to the point. For a puzzling confession, I can offer only a puzzling forgiveness.
ROMEO	In simple terms, I am in love with Capulet's daughter. I love her; she loves me. Together, we need you to perform a wedding. When, where, and how we met, courted, and promised to marry I will tell you along the way. Please promise to perform the ceremony today.

TRANSLATION

FRIAR	Holy Saint Francis! What a change is here!	65
	Is Rosaline, that thou didst love so dear,	
	So soon forsaken? Young men's love then lies	
	Not truly in their hearts, but in their eyes.	
	Jesu Maria! What a deal of brine	
	Hath washed thy sallow cheeks for Rosaline!	70
	How much salt water thrown away in waste	
	To season love, that of it doth not taste!	
	The sun not yet thy sighs from heaven clears,	
	Thy old groans ring yet in mine ancient ears.	
	Lo, here upon thy cheek the stain doth sit	75
	Of an old tear that is not washed off yet.	
	If e'er thou wast thyself, and these woes thine,	
	Thou and these woes were all for Rosaline.	
	And art thou changed? Pronounce this sentence then:	
	Women may fall when there's no strength in men.	80

ROMEO   Thou chid'st me oft for loving Rosaline.

FRIAR   For doting, not for loving, pupil mine.

ROMEO   And bad'st me bury love.

FRIAR   Not in a grave
           To lay one in, another out to have.

ROMEO   I pray thee chide not. She whom I love now   85
           Doth grace for grace and love for love allow.
           The other did not so.

FRIAR   O, she knew well
           Thy love did read by rote, that could not spell.
           But come, young waverer, come go with me.
           In one respect I'll thy assistant be;   90
           For this alliance may so happy prove
           To turn your households' rancor to pure love.

ROMEO   O, let us hence! I stand on sudden haste.

FRIAR   Wisely and slow. They stumble that run fast.
           [Exeunt]

FRIAR	Holy Saint Francis! You have changed! Have you so soon abandoned Rosaline, your former love? Youths' romances lie more in their eyes than in their hearts. Jesus son of Mary! What a sea of tears wet your pale cheeks for Rosaline! You have wasted a lot of seawater as a seasoning for romance, which you didn't even taste! Your sighs are still echoing in the sky. My ears still hear your groans. See, here on your cheek is a tear stain you haven't washed off yet. If it was really you and your troubles were really yours, they were for Rosaline. Have you changed? Repeat these words: Women fall when men are weak.
ROMEO	You scolded me often for loving Rosaline.
FRIAR	For infatuation, not for love, my pupil.
ROMEO	You wanted me to bury my feelings.
FRIAR	Not to put one romance in the grave and take another one out.
ROMEO	Don't scold me. My current love returns my love equally. Rosaline did not.
FRIAR	Rosaline knew that you mouthed sweet words without understanding their meaning. Come, young uncertain lover. For one reason, I will help you. This romance may be so beneficial that it will turn a family feud into pure harmony.
ROMEO	Let's hurry. I am in a rush.
FRIAR	Go wisely and slowly. If you run too fast, you will stumble. *[They go out]*

ACT II

TRANSLATION

ACT II, SCENE 4

The same. A street.

[Enter BENVOLIO and MERCUTIO]

MERCUTIO	Where the devil should this Romeo be? Came he not home to-night?
BENVOLIO	Not to his father's. I spoke with his man.
MERCUTIO	Why, that same pale hard-hearted wench, that Rosaline, Torments him so that he will sure run mad. 5
BENVOLIO	Tybalt, the kinsman to old Capulet, Hath sent a letter to his father's house.
MERCUTIO	A challenge, on my life.
BENVOLIO	Romeo will answer it.
MERCUTIO	Any man that can write may answer a letter. 10
BENVOLIO	Nay, he will answer the letter's master, how he dares, being dared.
MERCUTIO	Alas, poor Romeo, he is already dead! stabbed with a white wench's black eye; run through the ear with a love song; the very pin of his heart cleft 15 with the blind bow-boy's butt-shaft; and is he a man to encounter Tybalt?
BENVOLIO	Why, what is Tybalt?
MERCUTIO	More than Prince of Cats, I can tell you. O, he's the courageous captain of compliments. He 20 fights as you sing pricksong—keeps time, distance, and proportion; he rests his minim rests, one, two, and the third in your bosom! The very butcher of a silk button, a duellist, a duellist! a gentleman of the very first house, of the first and second cause. Ah, 25 the immortal passado! The punto reverso! The hay!
BENVOLIO	The what?

ACT II, SCENE 4

The same morning. A street in Verona.

[Enter BENVOLIO and MERCUTIO]

MERCUTIO	Where could Romeo be? Didn't he come home last night?
BENVOLIO	Not to his father's house. I asked Mr. Capulet.
MERCUTIO	Rosaline, that hard-hearted wench, tortures Romeo to madness.
BENVOLIO	Tybalt, the nephew of old Capulet, has sent a letter to Romeo's house.
MERCUTIO	I'll wager it was a challenge to a duel.
BENVOLIO	Romeo will answer him.
MERCUTIO	Anybody who can write can answer a letter.
BENVOLIO	No. I mean that Romeo will answer Tybalt's challenge by taking the dare.
MERCUTIO	Poor Romeo, he might as well be dead! Stabbed with a fair girl's glance; run through the ear with a love song; split through the core of his heart by Cupid's arrow. And is Romeo man enough to fight Tybalt?
BENVOLIO	What makes Tybalt special?
MERCUTIO	Tybalt is more than Prince of Cats in the animal fable. He is a bold captain when it comes to compliments. He fights in the rhythm of a song—he keeps time, distance, and a proportional response to each blow. He rests according to the rhythm—one, two, and the third count a thrust to your chest! He destroys buttons because he is a duelist! A top-ranked swordsman, an expert who is quick to take offense. He steps forward, thrusts with his backhand, and strikes the mark!
BENVOLIO	What?

TRANSLATION

MERCUTIO	The pox of such antic, lisping, affecting fantasticoes—these new tuners of accent! 'By Jesu, a very good blade! a very tall man! a very good whore!' Why, is not this a lamentable thing, grandsir, that we should be thus afflicted with these strange flies, these fashion-mongers, these pardon-me's, who stand so much on the new form that they cannot sit at ease on the old bench? O, their bones, their bones! *[Enter ROMEO]*
BENVOLIO	Here comes Romeo! here comes Romeo!
MERCUTIO	Without his roe, like a dried herring. O flesh, flesh, how art thou fishified! Now is he for the numbers that Petrarch flowed in. Laura, to his lady, was a kitchen wench (marry, she had a better love to berhyme her), Dido a dowdy, Cleopatra a gypsy, Helen and Hero hildings and harlots, Thisbe a grey eye or so, but not to the purpose. Signior Romeo, bonjour! There's a French salutation to your French slop. You gave us the counterfeit fairly last night.
ROMEO	Good morrow to you both. What counterfeit did I give you?
MERCUTIO	The slip, sir, the slip. Can you not conceive?
ROMEO	Pardon, good Mercutio. My business was great, and in such a case as mine a man may strain courtesy.
MERCUTIO	That's as much as to say, such a case as yours constrains a man to bow in the hams.
ROMEO	Meaning, to curtsy.
MERCUTIO	Thou hast most kindly hit it.
ROMEO	A most courteous exposition.
MERCUTIO	Nay, I am the very pink of courtesy.
ROMEO	Pink for flower.
MERCUTIO	Right.
ROMEO	Why, then is my pump well-flowered.

Line numbers: 30, 35, 40, 45, 50, 55, 60

MERCUTIO	A plague on prancing, lisping, posturing pretenders, those who are new to dueling. "By Jesus, a good dueler, a brave man, a good harlot!" It is obnoxious that these imposters, these fashionable, over-nice upstarts are so busy being stylish that they can't be comfortable with traditions. Oh, their bones! *[ROMEO enters]*
BENVOLIO	Here comes Romeo!
MERCUTIO	Without his doe, like a shriveled herring. Oh flesh, how you are fishified! He now chooses the rhythms of Petrarch's sonnets. Compared to Romeo's girl, Laura was a kitchen maid (she had a better poet to put her into poems), Dido was dowdy, Cleopatra a gypsy, Helen and Hero were sluts and harlots, Thisbe was gray-eyed, but of no use to Romeo. Mr. Romeo, bonjour! That's a French greeting for your French trousers. You gave us the slip last night.
ROMEO	Good morning. How did I deceive you?
MERCUTIO	The slip, sir, the slip. Don't you get it?
ROMEO	Forgive me, Mercutio. I had business to attend to. In such instances, a man may abandon good manners.
MERCUTIO	That is to say that, in such a case, a man may bow from the knees.
ROMEO	You mean "curtsy" like a woman?
MERCUTIO	I think you've got it.
ROMEO	A courteous explanation.
MERCUTIO	I am the very bloom of good manners.
ROMEO	A pink is a flower.
MERCUTIO	Right.
ROMEO	Well, then, my dress shoe is well pinked with holes.

ACT II

TRANSLATION

MERCUTIO	Sure wit, follow me this jest now till thou hast worn out thy pump, that, when the single sole of it is worn, the jest may remain, after the wearing, solely singular.	
ROMEO	O single-soled jest, solely singular for the singleness!	65
MERCUTIO	Come between us, good Benvolio! My wits faint.	
ROMEO	Swits and spurs, swits and spurs! or I'll cry a match.	
MERCUTIO	Nay, if our wits run the wild-goose chase, I am done; for thou hast more of the wild goose in one of thy wits than, I am sure, I have in my whole five. Was I with you there for the goose?	70
ROMEO	Thou wast never with me for anything when thou wast not there for the goose.	
MERCUTIO	I will bite thee by the ear for that jest.	
ROMEO	Nay, good goose, bite not!	75
MERCUTIO	Thy wit is a very bitter sweeting; it is a most sharp sauce.	
ROMEO	And is it not, then, well served in to a sweet goose?	
MERCUTIO	O, here's a wit of cheveril, that stretches from an inch narrow to an ell broad!	80
ROMEO	I stretch it out for that word 'broad,' which, added to the goose, proves thee far and wide a broad goose.	
MERCUTIO	Why, is not this better now than groaning for love? Now art thou sociable, now art thou Romeo; now art thou what thou art, by art as well as by nature. For this drivelling love is like a great natural that runs lolling up and down to hide his bauble in a hole.	85
BENVOLIO	Stop there, stop there!	
MERCUTIO	Thou desirest me to stop in my tale against the hair.	
BENVOLIO	Thou wouldst else have made thy tale large.	90
MERCUTIO	O, thou art deceived! I would have made it short; for I was come to the whole depth of my tale, and meant indeed to occupy the argument no longer.	

MERCUTIO	If you will follow my logic until you have worn out your dancing slipper, then, when the thin sole is worn through, the joke will remain, after the wearing, as bare feet.
ROMEO	A thin joke, a bare foot for its thinness.
MERCUTIO	Stand between us, Benvolio! My wittiness withers.
ROMEO	Let's continue swapping witty phrases and jabs or I will demand a contest.
MERCUTIO	If our wit runs wild, I quit. You have more wild goose in your wit than I have in my five senses. Did you get the point about the goose?
ROMEO	You have never been with me that you didn't goose me.
MERCUTIO	I will bite your ear for that joke.
ROMEO	Good goose, don't bite me!
MERCUTIO	Your wit is sweet-and-sour; it is a sharp accompaniment.
ROMEO	Isn't my wit a good accompaniment for a sweet goose?
MERCUTIO	Here's a piece of kidskin that stretches from an inch to forty-five inches wide.
ROMEO	I stretch it out and add "broad" to "goose," which proves you an obvious ninny.
MERCUTIO	Is that not better than being a groaning lover? Now you are sociable. Now you are the Romeo that you used to be. You are the real thing, just as nature made you. When you moon over romance, you act like a big idiot that waddles up and down to plunge his stick in a hole.
BENVOLIO	Halt there!
MERCUTIO	You want me to halt my story against the grain.
BENVOLIO	If I don't stop you, your tale will be too long.
MERCUTIO	You are tricked. I would have made a short tale. If I went to the far end of the tale, I would have exceeded our quibble.

ACT II

TRANSLATION

ROMEO	Here's goodly gear!	95
	[*Enter NURSE and her Man PETER*]	
MERCUTIO	A sail, a sail!	
BENVOLIO	Two, two! a shirt and a smock.	
NURSE	Peter!	
PETER	Anon.	
NURSE	My fan, Peter.	100
MERCUTIO	Good Peter, to hide her face; for her fan's the fairer face.	
NURSE	God ye good morrow, gentlemen.	
MERCUTIO	God ye good-den, fair gentlewoman.	
NURSE	Is it good-den?	105
MERCUTIO	'Tis no less, I tell ye; for the bawdy hand of the dial is now upon the prick of noon.	
NURSE	Out upon you! What a man are you!	
ROMEO	One, gentlewoman, that God hath made for himself to mar.	110
NURSE	By my troth, it is well said. 'For himself to mar,' quoth 'a? Gentlemen, can any of you tell me where I may find the young Romeo?	
ROMEO	I can tell you; but young Romeo will be older when you have found him than he was when you sought him. I am the youngest of that name, for fault of a worse.	115
NURSE	You say well.	
MERCUTIO	Yea, is the worst well? Very well took, i' faith! wisely, wisely.	
NURSE	If you be he, sir, I desire some confidence with you.	120
BENVOLIO	She will endite him to some supper.	
MERCUTIO	A bawd, a bawd, a bawd! So ho!	
ROMEO	What hast thou found?	

ROMEO	Here is an interesting costume! *[Enter NURSE and her Man, PETER]*
MERCUTIO	A sail!
BENVOLIO	Two sails! A man's shirt and a woman's overshirt.
NURSE	Peter!
PETER	At once.
NURSE	Bring my fan, Peter.
MERCUTIO	Good Peter, bring the fan to hide her face, for the fan is more attractive.
NURSE	God give you a good morning, gentlemen.
MERCUTIO	God give you a good evening, ma'am.
NURSE	Is it afternoon already?
MERCUTIO	It is. I assure you, the vulgar hand of the clock is on the prick of noon.
NURSE	Away with you! What kind of man are you!
ROMEO	A man, ma'am, that God made to ruin himself.
NURSE	Well put. Did he say "To ruin himself"? Gentlemen, can you tell me where to look for Romeo?
ROMEO	I can tell you. You talk so much that Romeo will be older when you find him than when you looked for him. Romeo is my name. It could have been worse.
NURSE	Well said.
MERCUTIO	Is the worst word well put? Very well taken! Wisely, wisely.
NURSE	If you are Romeo, I want to speak privately with you.
BENVOLIO	She will invite him to dinner.
MERCUTIO	A procurer of prostitutes! Oho!
ROMEO	What do you know about the nurse?

TRANSLATION

MERCUTIO	No hare, sir; unless a hare, sir, in a lenten pie, that is something stale and hoar ere it be spent. 125 *[He walks by them and sings]*

> *An old hare hoar,*
> *And an old hare hoar,*
> *Is very good meat in Lent;*
> *But a hare that is hoar*
> *Is too much for a score*   130
> *When it hoars ere it be spent.*

	Romeo, will you come to your father's? We'll to dinner thithcr.
ROMEO	I will follow you.
MERCUTIO	Farewell, ancient lady. Farewell. *[Sings]* lady, lady, lady. 135 *[Exeunt MERCUTIO, BENVOLIO]*
NURSE	I pray you, sir, what saucy merchant was this that was so full of his ropery?
ROMEO	A gentleman, nurse, that loves to hear himself talk and will speak more in a minute than he will stand to in a month. 140
NURSE	An 'a speak anything against me, I'll take him down, an 'a were lustier than he is, and twenty such Jacks; and if I cannot, I'll find those that shall. Scurvy knave! I am none of his flirt-gills; I am none of his skains-mates. And thou must stand by too, and 145 suffer every knave to use me at his pleasure!
PETER	I saw no man use you at his pleasure. If I had, my weapon should quickly have been out, I warrant you. I dare draw as soon as another man, if I see occasion in a good quarrel, and the law on my side. 150
NURSE	Now, afore God, I am so vexed that every part about me quivers. Scurvy knave! Pray you, sir, a word; and, as I told you, my young lady bid me inquire you out. What she bid me say, I will keep to myself; but first let me tell ye, if ye should lead her into a fool's 155 paradise, as they say, it were a very gross kind of behavior, as they say; for the gentlewoman is young; and therefore, if you should deal double with her, truly it were an ill thing to be offered to any gentlewoman, and very weak dealing. 160

MERCUTIO	Not a slut, sir, unless a hare fit for an Easter pie is old and moldy before it is all eaten. *[He walks by them and sings]*

An old moldy rabbit,
And an old moldy rabbit,
Is very good meat before Lent;
But a rabbit that is moldy
Is too much for twenty diners
When it molds before it is eaten.

Romeo, will you return to your father's house? We'll come to dinner there.

ROMEO	I will follow you.
MERCUTIO	Farewell, old lady. Goodbye. *[He sings]* Lady, lady, lady. *[MERCUTIO and BENVOLIO depart]*
NURSE	Who was that impertinent fellow that was so roguish?
ROMEO	Nurse, Mercutio is a man who loves to hear himself chatter. He can say more in a minute than he can explain in a month.
NURSE	If he defames me, I'll pounce on him, even if he were stronger and surrounded by twenty such quipsters. And if I can't handle him, I'll find someone to help me. Scroungy rascal! I'm no slut; I'm no loose woman. And you just stand there and let every ruffian abuse me for fun!
PETER	I didn't see anyone abuse you for fun. If I had, I would have whipped out my weapon, I guarantee you. I draw my sword as soon as anybody, if I see a good argument brewing and if the law is on my side.
NURSE	Well, I am so agitated that I'm all a-quiver. Scroungy rascal! Please, sir, I want a word with you. As I told you, Juliet asked me to look for you. What she asked me to say I will keep to myself. But I warn you, if you should deceive her, you would be guilty of disgusting behavior. Juliet is young. If you trick her, you would be wronging a polite woman. You would be taking advantage of her.

ACT II

TRANSLATION

| ROMEO | Nurse, commend me to thy lady and mistress. |
| | I protest unto thee— |

| NURSE | Good heart, and i' faith I will tell her as much. |
| | Lord, Lord! she will be a joyful woman. |

| ROMEO | What wilt thou tell her, nurse? Thou dost not | 165 |
| | mark me. |

| NURSE | I will tell her, sir, that you do protest, which, as |
| | I take it, is a gentlemanlike offer. |

ROMEO	Bid her devise
	Some means to come to shrift this afternoon;	170
	And there she shall at Friar Laurence' cell
	Be shrived and married. Here is for thy pains.

| NURSE | No, truly, sir; not a penny. |

| ROMEO | Go to! I say you shall. |

| NURSE | This afternoon, sir? Well, she shall be there. | 175 |

ROMEO	And stay, good nurse, behind the abbey wall.
	Within this hour my man shall be with thee
	And bring thee cords made like a tackled stair,
	Which to the high topgallant of my joy
	Must be my convoy in the secret night.	180
	Farewell. Be trusty, and I'll quit thy pains.
	Farewell. Commend me to thy mistress.

| NURSE | Now God in heaven bless thee! Hark you, sir. |

| ROMEO | What say'st thou, my dear nurse? |

| NURSE | Is your man secret? Did you ne'er hear say, | 185 |
| | Two may keep counsel, putting one away? |

| ROMEO | I warrant thee my man's as true as steel. |

NURSE	Well, sir, my mistress is the sweetest lady. Lord,
	Lord! when 'twas a little prating thing—O, there is a
	nobleman in town, one Paris, that would fain	190
	lay knife aboard; but she, good soul, had as lieve see
	a toad, a very toad, as see him. I anger her sometimes,
	and tell her that Paris is the properer man; but I'll
	warrant you, when I say so, she looks as pale as any clout
	in the versal world. Doth not rosemary and Romeo	195
	begin both with a letter?

ORIGINAL

ROMEO	Nurse, give my regards to Juliet. I assure you—
NURSE	My good man, I will tell her. Lord! She will be joyous.
ROMEO	What will you tell her, nurse? You haven't heard me say anything.
NURSE	I will tell her that you make what I assume to be a gentlemanly offer.
ROMEO	Have her think up a reason to come to confession this afternoon. And there at Friar Laurence's room, she will be forgiven and married. Here is a reward for your errand.
NURSE	No, sir. I won't take a penny.
ROMEO	Hush! You will take it.
NURSE	This afternoon, sir? She will meet you there.
ROMEO	Good nurse, wait behind the abbey wall. Within an hour my servant will bring you a rope ladder by which I will climb to my happiness for a private night of love. Goodbye. Be faithful to me and I will reward you. Goodbye. Give my regards to Juliet.
NURSE	May God bless you! One more thing, sir.
ROMEO	What is it, dear nurse?
NURSE	Can I trust your servant? Haven't you heard it said that two can keep a secret if one is dead?
ROMEO	I promise you that my servant is as trustworthy as steel.
NURSE	Sir, Juliet is the sweetest girl. Lord, when she was a babbling baby—there is a nobleman in Verona named Paris who would have Juliet. She, good soul, would rather view a toad as look at him. It angers her when I tell her that Paris is the more handsome man. I guarantee you, when I compliment him, she turns pale as any cloth in the world. Don't rosemary and Romeo both begin with an R?

ACT II

TRANSLATION

ROMEO	Ay, nurse; what of that? Both with an R.
NURSE	Ah, mocker! That's the dog's name. R is for the— No; I know it begins with some other letter; and she hath the prettiest sententious of it, of you and rosemary, 200 that it would do you good to hear it.
ROMEO	Commend me to thy lady.
NURSE	Ay, a thousand times. *[Exit ROMEO]* Peter!
PETER	Anon.
NURSE	Peter, take my fan, and go before, and apace. 205 *[Exit after PETER]*

ROMEO	Both begin with an R. So what?
NURSE	You mock me! R-r-r-r is the sound of a dog's growl. R is for the— No, I know it starts with some other letter. She makes the prettiest sentences about you and rosemary. It would gladden you to hear her.
ROMEO	Give my regards to Juliet.
NURSE	Yes, a thousand times. *[ROMEO goes out]* Peter!
PETER	At your service.
NURSE	Peter, take my fan, lead the way and quickly. *[She goes out, following PETER]*

ACT II

TRANSLATION

ACT II, SCENE 5

The same. Capulet's garden.

[Enter JULIET]

JULIET   The clock struck nine when I did send the nurse;
In half an hour she promised to return.
Perchance she cannot meet him. That's not so.
O, she is lame! Love's heralds should be thoughts,
Which ten times faster glide than the sun's beams   5
Driving back shadows over low'ring hills.
Therefore do nimble-pinioned doves draw Love,
And therefore hath the wind-swift Cupid wings.
Now is the sun upon the highmost hill
Of this day's journey, and from nine till twelve   10
Is three long hours; yet she is not come.
Had she affections and warm youthful blood,
She would be as swift in motion as a ball;
My words would bandy her to my sweet love,
And his to me.   15
But old folks, many feign as they were dead—
Unwieldly, slow, heavy and pale as lead.
[Enter NURSE and PETER].
O God, she comes! O honey nurse, what news?
Hast thou met with him? Send thy man away.

NURSE   Peter, stay at the gate. *[Exit PETER]*   20

JULIET   Now, good sweet nurse—O Lord, why lookest thou sad?
Though news be sad, yet tell them merrily;
If good, thou shamest the music of sweet news
By playing it to me with so sour a face.

NURSE   I am aweary, give me leave awhile.   25
Fie, how my bones ache! What a jaunce have I had!

JULIET   I would thou hadst my bones, and I thy news.
Nay, come, I pray thee speak. Good, good nurse, speak.

NURSE   Jesu, what haste! Can you not stay awhile?
Do you not see that I am out of breath?   30

ORIGINAL

ACT II, SCENE 5

The same morning. Capulet's garden.

[Enter JULIET]

JULIET   The clock struck 9:00 A.M. when I sent the nurse on her errand. She promised to return in a half hour. Maybe she didn't find him. No, it can't be. Oh, she is a poor choice of messenger! Love's messengers should be thoughts, which slip ten times faster over shadowy hills than sunbeams. That is why agile-winged doves pull the chariot of Venus and why Cupid has swift wings. The sun is high. I have waited three long hours, from 9:00 A.M. until noon. But she has not come. If she were young and tenderhearted, she would be as fast as a ball. My word would toss her to my sweet Romeo and his words would toss her back to me. But old people pretend to be dead—awkward, slow, heavy, and colorless as lead. *[Enter NURSE and PETER]* Oh God, she is here! Oh sweet nurse, what news do you bring? Have you met Romeo? Send Peter away.

NURSE   Peter, stand by the gate. *[PETER goes out]*

JULIET   Oh good nurse—Oh Lord, why do you look sad? If you bring sad news, relate it cheerfully. If you bring good news, you destroy the pleasant words by speaking them with a sour face.

NURSE   I am tired, let me rest a minute. Drat, how my bones ache! What a trudge I had in Verona.

JULIET   I would trade you my bones for your news. Please, tell me. Good nurse, speak.

NURSE   Jesus, why the hurry! Can you not wait a minute? Don't you see that I am out of breath?

TRANSLATION

JULIET	How art thou out of breath when thou hast breath To say to me that thou art out of breath? The excuse that thou dost make in this delay Is longer than the tale thou dost excuse. Is thy news good or bad? Answer to that. 35 Say either, and I'll stay the circumstance. Let me be satisfied, is't good or bad?
NURSE	Well, you have made a simple choice; you know not how to choose a man. Romeo? No, not he. Though his face be better than any man's, yet his leg excels all 40 men's; and for a hand and a foot, and a body, though they be not to be talked on, yet they are past compare. He is not the flower of courtesy, but, I'll warrant him, as gentle as a lamb. Go thy ways, wench; serve God. What, have you dined at home? 45
JULIET	No, no. But all this did I know before. What says he of our marriage? What of that?
NURSE	Lord, how my head aches! What a head have I! It beats as it would fall in twenty pieces. My back a t' other side—ah, my back, my back! 50 Beshrew your heart for sending me about To catch my death with jauncing up and down!
JULIET	I' faith, I am sorry that thou art not well. Sweet, sweet, sweet nurse, tell me, what says my love?
NURSE	Your love says, like an honest gentleman, 55 and a courteous, and kind, and handsome, and, I warrant, a virtuous—Where is your mother?
JULIET	Where is my mother? Why, she is within. Where should she be? How oddly thou repliest! 'Your love says, like an honest gentleman, 60 "Where is your mother?"'
NURSE	O God's Lady dear! Are you so hot? Marry come up, I trow. Is this the poultice for my aching bones? Henceforward do your messages yourself.
JULIET	Here's such a coil! Come, what says Romeo? 65
NURSE	Have you got leave to go to shrift today?
JULIET	I have.

ORIGINAL

JULIET	How can you be breathless when you have enough breath to tell me you are breathless? The excuse you give is longer than the message you have for me. Is your news good or bad? Tell me. Say either "good" or "bad" and I'll wait for the details. Satisfy my curiosity, good or bad?
NURSE	Well, that is simple enough. You don't know how to choose a man. Romeo is not a good choice. Though he has a handsomer face than any man's and his leg outdoes all men, and in terms of hand, foot, and body, though they are not worth talking about, yet they are beyond compare. He is not a model of good manners, but I'll guarantee that he is as gentle as a lamb. Off with you, girl, to God's service. Have you had lunch?
JULIET	No. But I knew all this before. What did he say about marriage? Did he mention that?
NURSE	Lord, how my head pains me! I have such a headache! It throbs as though it would break into twenty pieces. On the other side of my back—oh, my back, my back! Curse your heart for sending me out to catch my death by trotting all over Verona.
JULIET	I am sorry you are not well. Sweet nurse, tell me, what did Romeo say?
NURSE	Your love says, like an honest gentleman and mannerly and kind and handsome, and, I guarantee, respectable— Where is your mother?
JULIET	Where is my mother? Why she is in the house. Where else would she be? How strangely you reply to my questions! "Your love says, like an honest gentleman, 'Where is your mother?'"
NURSE	By the Virgin Mary! Why are you so demanding? Ease up. Are your questions a cure for my aching bones? From now on, carry your own messages.
JULIET	What a mess! Hurry, tell me what Romeo said.
NURSE	Do you have permission to go to confession today?
JULIET	I have.

ACT II

TRANSLATION

NURSE   Then hie you hence to Friar Laurence' cell;
                       There stays a husband to make you a wife.
                       Now comes the wanton blood up in your cheeks: 70
                       They'll be in scarlet straight at any news.
                       Hie you to church; I must another way,
                       To fetch a ladder, by the which your love
                       Must climb a bird's nest soon when it is dark.
                       I am the drudge, and toil in your delight;   75
                       But you shall bear the burden soon at night.
                       Go; I'll to dinner; hie you to the cell.

JULIET   Hie to high fortune! Honest nurse farewell.
                       [Exeunt]

ORIGINAL

NURSE   Then hurry to Friar Laurence's room. There is a husband waiting to make you a wife. Now you blush. You would have red cheeks at any news of Romeo. Hurry to church. I am headed in another direction to find a rope ladder by which Romeo may climb to your room tonight. I must fetch and carry for you. But you shall bear his weight tonight. Go. I'll eat lunch. Hurry to Friar Laurence's room.

JULIET   Hurry to good fortune! Honest nurse, goodbye.
[They go out]

ACT II

ACT II, SCENE 6

The same. Friar Laurence's cell.

[Enter FRIAR LAURENCE and ROMEO]

FRIAR	So smile the heavens upon this holy act	
	That after-hours with sorrow chide us not!	
ROMEO	Amen, amen! But come what sorrow can,	
	It cannot countervail the exchange of joy	
	That one short minute gives me in her sight.	5
	Do thou but close our hands with holy words,	
	Then love-devouring death do what he dare—	
	It is enough I may but call her mine.	
FRIAR	These violent delights have violent ends	
	And in their triumph die, like fire and powder,	10
	Which, as they kiss, consume. The sweetest honey	
	Is loathsome in his own deliciousness	
	And in the taste confounds the appetite.	
	Therefore love moderately: long love doth so;	
	Too swift arrives as tardy as too slow.	15

[Enter JULIET]

	Here comes the lady. O, so light a foot	
	Will ne'er wear out the everlasting flint.	
	A lover may bestride the gossamer	
	That idles in the wanton summer air,	
	And yet not fall; so light is vanity.	20
JULIET	Good even to my ghostly confessor.	
FRIAR	Romeo shall thank thee, daughter, for us both.	
JULIET	As much to him, else is his thanks too much.	
ROMEO	Ah, Juliet, if the measure of thy joy	
	Be heaped like mine, and that thy skill be more	25
	To blazon it, then sweeten with thy breath	
	This neighbor air, and let rich music's tongue	
	Unfold the imagined happiness that both	
	Receive in either by this dear encounter.	

ORIGINAL

ACT II, SCENE 6

The same day. Friar Laurence's room.

[Enter FRIAR LAURENCE and ROMEO]

FRIAR   I hope heaven condones this marriage and doesn't blame us later!

ROMEO   Amen to that! But, whatever sorrow comes, it outweighs the shared joy I receive from one minute with Juliet. Join our hands with marriage vows. Whatever death may do to destroy love, I will be content when Juliet is my wife.

FRIAR   These emotional joys have emotional conclusions. They die at the moment of triumph. Like fire igniting gunpowder, romance can consume lovers from the effects of one kiss. The sweetest honey is unpleasant for its strong flavor. Too much sweetness can be unbearable. So, love moderately. A long romance requires self-control. Too swift a union of lovers is as harmful as a delayed union. *[Enter JULIET]* Here comes the bride. Oh, so light is her step that she would never wear down stone. A lover may walk on a spider's web that riffles in the summer air and yet not fall off. So insubstantial is mortal joy.

JULIET   Good afternoon to my spiritual counselor.

FRIAR   Romeo will return the greeting, daughter, for both him and me.

JULIET   Good afternoon to Romeo, else his thanks for the two of you is too much.

ROMEO   Oh Juliet, if your joy is piled as high as mine and if you be more skillful in announcing it, then sweeten your words with this comment. Let your words express the anticipated happiness to us both in this precious ceremony.

TRANSLATION

JULIET	Conceit, more rich in matter than in words,	30
	Brags of his substance, not of ornament.	
	They are but beggars that can count their worth;	
	But my true love is grown to such excess	
	I cannot sum up sum of half my wealth.	
FRIAR	Come, come with me, and we will make short work;	35
	For, by your leaves, you shall not stay alone	
	Till Holy Church incorporate two in one.	
	[Exeunt]	

JULIET   Imagination, which is richer in ideas than in words, boasts of meaning, not of decoration. Those who sum up their worth are only beggars. But my love for you has grown so great that I can't total up half my wealth.

FRIAR   Come with me and we will quickly complete the marriage ceremony. For, if you are willing, I will not leave you unchaperoned until the holy sacrament makes you man and wife. *[They go out]*

ACT II

ACT III, SCENE 1

Verona. A public place.

[Enter MERCUTIO, BENVOLIO, and Men]

BENVOLIO	I pray thee, good Mercutio, let's retire.
	The day is hot, the Capulets abroad,
	And, if we meet, we shall not 'scape a brawl,
	For now, these hot days, is the mad blood stirring.

MERCUTIO Thou are like one of these fellows that, when   5
he enters the confines of a tavern, claps me his sword
upon the table and says 'God send me no need of thee!'
and by the operation of the second cup draws him on the
drawer, when indeed there is no need.

BENVOLIO Am I like such a fellow?   10

MERCUTIO Come, come, thou art as hot a Jack in thy
mood as any in Italy; and as soon moved to be moody,
and as soon moody to be moved.

BENVOLIO And what to?

MERCUTIO Nay, and there were two such, we should   15
have none shortly, for one would kill the other. Thou!
why, thou wilt quarrel with a man that hath a hair
more or a hair less in his beard than thou hast. Thou
wilt quarrel with a man for cracking nuts, having no
other reason but because thou hast hazel eyes. What   20
eye but such an eye would spy out such a quarrel? Thy
head is as full of quarrels as an egg is full of
meat; and yet thy head hath been beaten as addle as
an egg for quarrelling. Thou hast quarrelled with a man for
coughing in the street, because he hath wakened thy   25
dog that hath lain asleep in the sun. Didst thou not fall
out with a tailor for wearing his new doublet before
Easter? With another for tying his new shoes with old
riband? And yet thou wilt tutor me from quarrelling!

BENVOLIO An I were so apt to quarrel as thou art, any   30
man should buy the fee simple of my life for an hour
and a quarter.

MERCUTIO The fee simple? O simple!
[Enter TYBALT and others]

BENVOLIO By my head, here come the Capulets.

ACT III, SCENE 1

Verona. A public place.

[Enter MERCUTIO, BENVOLIO, and Men]

BENVOLIO	Please, Mercutio, let's go home. It is hot today and the Capulets are on the streets. If we encounter them, we can't avoid a brawl. On these hot summer days, recklessness is stirring.
MERCUTIO	You are like a guy who enters a bar, plunks his sword on the table, and says, "God give me no reason to use you!" After the guy's second drink, he menaces the barman when there is no call for a fight.
BENVOLIO	Am I like that?
MERCUTIO	Yes. You are as feisty a fellow in your current mood as anyone in Italy. You are as quickly roused to anger as you are ill tempered enough to be provoked.
BENVOLIO	Provoked to what?
MERCUTIO	If there were two as feisty as you, they would soon dwindle to none, for one would kill the other. You! Why, you would quarrel with a man for having one more or one less hair in his beard than you. You would pick a fight with a man for cracking hazelnuts and give no other reason than that your eyes are hazel. Only an eye like yours can spy a quarrel at hand. Your head is as spiteful as an egg is full of food. Your head has been beaten as frothy as an egg for your quarreling. You have argued with a man for coughing in the street because he woke up your dog that was sleeping in the sun. Didn't you provoke a fight with a tailor for wearing his new vest before Easter? And with another man for tying his shoes with old laces? And yet you will scold me about arguing!
BENVOLIO	If I were as quarrelsome as you, anyone could have my life in an hour and a quarter.
MERCUTIO	He could buy the simple deed? You simpleton! *[Enter TYBALT and others]*
BENVOLIO	By my head, here come the Capulets.

ACT III

TRANSLATION

| MERCUTIO | By my heel, I care not. | 35 |

TYBALT Follow me close, for I will speak to them.
Gentlemen, good-den. A word with one of you.

MERCUTIO And but one word with one of us?
Couple it with something; make it a word and a blow.

TYBALT You shall find me apt enough to that, sir, an   40
you will give me occasion.

MERCUTIO Could you not take some occasion
without giving?

TYBALT Mercutio, thou consortest with Romeo.

MERCUTIO Consort? What, dost thou make us minstrels?   45
An thou make minstrels of us, look to hear
Nothing but discords. Here's my fiddlestick; here's
that shall make you dance. Zounds, consort!

BENVOLIO We talk here in the public haunt of men.
Either withdraw unto some private place,   50
Or reason coldly of your grievances,
Or else depart. Here all eyes gaze on us.

MERCUTIO Men's eyes were made to look, and let them gaze.
I will not budge for no man's pleasure, I.
[Enter ROMEO]

TYBALT Well, peace be with you, sir. Here comes my man.   55

MERCUTIO But I'll be hanged, sir, if he wear your livery.
Marry, go before to field, he'll be your follower!
Your worship in that sense may call him man.

TYBALT Romeo, the love I bear thee can afford
No better term than this: thou art a villain.   60

ROMEO Tybalt, the reason that I have to love thee
Doth much excuse the appertaining rage
To such a greeting. Villain am I none.
Therefore farewell. I see thou knowest me not.

TYBALT Boy, this shall not excuse the injuries   65
That thou hast done me; therefore turn and draw.

ROMEO I do protest I never injured thee,
But love thee better than thou canst devise
Till thou shalt know the reason of my love;
And so, good Capulet, which name I tender   70
As dearly as mine own, be satisfied.

ORIGINAL

MERCUTIO	By my heel, I don't care.
TYBALT	*[To the Capulet followers]* Stick with me. I will address them. *[To the Montagues]* Gentlemen, good afternoon. May I have a word with one of you.
MERCUTIO	Only one word with one of us Montagues? Add something else—a word and a punch.
TYBALT	You will find me capable enough for fighting, sir, if you give me reason to fight.
MERCUTIO	Would you dare us to fight?
TYBALT	Mercutio, you consort with Romeo.
MERCUTIO	Consort? Do you call us musicians? If you think we are musicians, expect nothing but disharmony. Here is my fiddlestick—here's a blade that will make you dance. By God's wounds, consort!
BENVOLIO	We are talking in a public place. Either move to a private place or settle your squabble without anger or else leave town. Everybody is looking at us here.
MERCUTIO	People are meant to watch. Let them look. I won't leave to accommodate anybody. *[Enter ROMEO]*
TYBALT	Well, forget the fight. Here comes the man I am waiting for.
MERCUTIO	Well I'd be amazed, Tybalt, if Romeo were your servant. Take the battleground and he will follow you! In challenging him, you will face a man.
TYBALT	Romeo, in my opinion, you are no better than a felon.
ROMEO	Tybalt, the reason that I admire you will end our enmity. I am not a criminal. Goodbye. I see that you don't understand our new relationship.
TYBALT	Boy, your comment can't excuse your past injury to me. So, turn and draw your sword.
ROMEO	I declare that I never harmed you. I have reason to honor you, but I can't tell you why. And so be content, good Capulet, a name I mention as dearly as I do Montague.

ACT III

TRANSLATION

MERCUTIO	O calm, dishonorable, vile submission! Alla stoccata carries it away. *[Draws]* Tybalt, you ratcatcher, will you walk?
TYBALT	What wouldst thou have with me? 75
MERCUTIO	Good King of Cats, nothing but one of your nine lives. That I mean to make bold withal, and, as you shall use me hereafter, dry-beat the rest of the eight. Will you pluck your sword out of his pilcher by the ears? Make haste, lest mine be about your ears ere it be out. 80
TYBALT	I am for you. *[Draws]*
ROMEO	Gentle Mercutio, put thy rapier up.
MERCUTIO	Come, sir, your passado! *[They fight]*
ROMEO	Draw, Benvolio; beat down their weapons. Gentlemen, for shame! forbear this outrage! 85 Tybalt, Mercutio, the Prince expressly hath Forbid this bandying in Verona streets. Hold Tybalt! Good Mercutio! *[TYBALT under ROMEO'S arm thrusts MERCUTIO in,* *and flies with his Followers]*
MERCUTIO	I am hurt. A plague o' both your houses! I am sped. Is he gone and hath nothing?
BENVOLIO	What, art thou hurt? 90
MERCUTIO	Ay, ay, a scratch, a scratch. Marry, 'tis enough. Where is my page? Go, villain, fetch a surgeon. *[Exit Page]*
ROMEO	Courage, man. The hurt cannot be much.
MERCUTIO	No, 'tis not so deep as a well, nor so wide as a church door; but 'tis enough, 'twill serve. Ask for 95 me to-morrow, and you shall find me a grave man. I am peppered, I warrant, for this world. A plague o' both your houses! Zounds, a dog, a rat, a mouse, a cat, to scratch a man to death! a braggart, a rogue, a villain, that fights by the book of arithmetic! Why the devil 100 came you between us? I was hurt under your arm.
ROMEO	I thought all for the best.

MERCUTIO	What a calm, dishonorable, and insufferable retreat! An exchange of sword thrusts is needed here. *[MERCUTIO draws his sword against TYBALT]* Tybalt, you rat catcher, will you come with me?
TYBALT	What do you want with me?
MERCUTIO	Good King of Cats, I want one of your nine lives. I mean to take that one life and, depending on how you respond, I will pummel the other eight lives. Will you draw your sword from its scabbard? Hurry before I thrust mine around your ears before you are ready.
TYBALT	I am ready. *[Tybalt draws his sword]*
ROMEO	Mercutio, put up your sword.
MERCUTIO	Come, Tybalt, a strong thrust! *[They clash]*
ROMEO	Draw your sword, Benvolio. Ward off their weapons. Gentleman, this is shameful! Stop this outrageous behavior! Tybalt, Mercutio, Prince Escalus has forbidden brawling in Verona. Stop Tybalt! Stop Mercutio! *[TYBALT stabs MERCUTIO with one thrust under ROMEO's arm. TYBALT runs away with his followers]*
MERCUTIO	I am hit. A curse on the Capulets and Montagues! I am done for. Has Tybalt escaped without a scratch?
BENVOLIO	Are you hurt?
MERCUTIO	Yes, a scratch. But it is enough to kill me. Where is my servant? Go, you, and bring a surgeon. *[The page goes out]*
ROMEO	Be brave, man. You can't be hurt bad.
MERCUTIO	No, the wound is not as deep as a well or as wide as a church door. But it is enough to kill me. It will do. Look for me tomorrow and you will find me in the cemetery. I am done for. I curse the Capulets and the Montagues. God's wounds, a dog, rat, mouse, or cat can scratch a man to death! A boaster, rascal, criminal that fights with words! Why did you come between us? Tybalt thrust his sword under your arm and into me.
ROMEO	I meant to stop the fight.

ACT III

MERCUTIO	Help me into some house, Benvolio, Or I shall faint. A plague o' both your houses! They have made worms' meat of me. I have it, 105 And soundly too. Your houses! *[Exit, supported by BENVOLIO]*
ROMEO	This gentleman, the Prince's near ally, My very friend, hath got this mortal hurt In my behalf—my reputation stained With Tybalt's slander—Tybalt, that an hour 110 Hath been my cousin. O sweet Juliet, Thy beauty hath made me effeminate And in my temper soft'ned valor's steel! *[Enter BENVOLIO]*
BENVOLIO	O Romeo, Romeo, brave Mercutio is dead! That gallant spirit hath aspired the clouds, 115 Which too untimely here did scorn the earth.
ROMEO	This day's black fate on moe days doth depend; This but begins the woe others must end. *[Enter TYBALT]*
BENVOLIO	Here comes the furious Tybalt back again.
ROMEO	Alive in triumph, and Mercutio slain? 120 Away to heaven respective lenity, And fire-eyed fury be my conduct now! Now, Tybalt, take the 'villain' back again That late thou gavest me; for Mercutio's soul Is but a little way above our heads, 125 Staying for thine to keep him company. Either thou or I, or both, must go with him.
TYBALT	Thou, wretched boy, that didst consort him here, Shalt with him hence.
ROMEO	This shall determine that. *[They fight. TYBALT falls]*
BENVOLIO	Romeo, away, be gone! 130 The citizens are up, and Tybalt slain. Stand not amazed. The Prince will doom thee death If thou art taken. Hence, be gone, away!
ROMEO	O, I am fortune's fool!
BENVOLIO	Why dost thou stay? *[Exit ROMEO. Enter Citizens]*

ORIGINAL

MERCUTIO	Assist me into a house, Benvolio, or I will faint in the street. A curse on the Capulets and Montagues! They have turned me into food for worms. I've had it. I am soundly beaten. Curse your houses! *[BENVOLIO supports MERCUTIO as they depart]*
ROMEO	This man, a relative of Prince Escalus, my dear friend, was mortally wounded because of me—because Tybalt slandered my honor—Tybalt, who has been my cousin by marriage for only an hour. Oh sweet Juliet, your beauty has made me weak and less courageous! *[Enter BENVOLIO]*
BENVOLIO	Oh Romeo, brave Mercutio is dead! His gallant soul has risen from earth to heaven much too soon.
ROMEO	This terrible day will darken other days. This fatal duel has started a feud that other fighters must end. *[Enter TYBALT]*
BENVOLIO	Tybalt is back. He's furious.
ROMEO	Tybalt is victorious and Mercutio is dead? I rid myself of mildness and vow to be fired with fury! Now, Tybalt, take back the charge you leveled at me. Mercutio's spirit has just gone to heaven. It waits for your soul to keep it company. Either you or I or both must die with Mercutio.
TYBALT	You wretched boy who conspired here with Mercutio shall join him in death.
ROMEO	This sword will resolve the issue. *[They fight. TYBALT falls]*
BENVOLIO	Romeo, run. The citizens are angry and Tybalt is dead. Don't stand there and stare. Prince Escalus will condemn you to death if he finds you with the body. Hurry, go!
ROMEO	Oh, I am fortune's toy!
BENVOLIO	Why are you delaying? *[Exit ROMEO. Enter Citizens]*

ACT III

TRANSLATION

CITIZEN	Which way ran he that killed Mercutio? 135
	Tybalt, that murderer, which way ran he?
BENVOLIO	There lies that Tybalt.
CITIZEN	Up, sir, go with me.
	I charge thee in the Prince's name obey.
	[Enter PRINCE (attended), old MONTAGUE, CAPULET,
	their WIVES, and all]
PRINCE	Where are the vile beginners of this fray?
BENVOLIO	O noble Prince, I can discover all 140
	The unlucky manage of this fatal brawl.
	There lies the man, slain by young Romeo,
	That slew thy kinsman, brave Mercutio.
CAPULET'S WIFE	Tybalt, my cousin! O my brother's child!
	O Prince! O husband! O, the blood is spilled 145
	Of my dear kinsman! Prince, as thou art true,
	For blood of ours shed blood of Montague.
	O cousin, cousin!
PRINCE	Benvolio, who began this bloody fray?
BENVOLIO	Tybalt, here slain, whom Romeo's hand did slay. 150
	Romeo, that spoke him fair, bid him bethink
	How nice the quarrel was, and urged withal
	Your high displeasure. All this—uttered
	With gentle breath, calm look, knees humbly bowed—
	Could not take truce with the unruly spleen 155
	Of Tybalt deaf to peace, but that he tilts
	With piercing steel at bold Mercutio's breast;
	Who, all as hot, turns deadly point to point,
	And, with a martial scorn, with one hand beats
	Cold death aside and with the other sends 160
	It back to Tybalt, whose dexterity
	Retorts it. Romeo he cries aloud,
	'Hold, friends! friends, part!', and swifter than his tongue,
	His agile arm beats down their fatal points,
	And 'twixt them rushes; underneath whose arm 165
	An envious thrust from Tybalt hit the life
	Of stout Mercutio, and then Tybalt fled;
	But by and by comes back to Romeo,
	Who had but newly entertained revenge,
	And to't they go like lightning; for, ere I 170
	Could draw to part them, was stout Tybalt slain;
	And, as he fell, did Romeo turn and fly.
	This is the truth, or let Benvolio die.

CITIZEN	Which way did Mercutio's killer go? Which direction did the murdering Tybalt run?
BENVOLIO	There lies Tybalt's corpse.
CITIZEN	Come with me, sir. In the name of Prince Escalus, I charge you to obey me. *[Enter PRINCE (attended), old MONTAGUE, CAPULET, their WIVES, and all]*
PRINCE	Where are the vile scrappers of this fight?
BENVOLIO	Oh noble Prince, I can testify to the unfortunate nature of this deadly brawl. Romeo killed this man, Tybalt, who murdered your relative, Mercutio.
CAPULET'S WIFE	Tybalt, my nephew! Oh, my brother's child! Oh Prince Escalus! Oh my husband! Oh, my dear nephew is murdered. Prince, be true to your command. A Capulet killed a Montague. Oh kinsman, kinsman!
PRINCE	Benvolio, who started this brawl?
BENVOLIO	Tybalt, whom Romeo killed. Romeo spoke fairly to him and asked him to forego a trivial argument and urged Tybalt to remember your distaste for the family feud. All this Romeo said with gentle words, calm face, and bowed knees. He could not persuade Tybalt to settle the matter without violence. With uncontrolled anger, Tybalt remained deaf to persuasion. He thrust at Mercutio's chest a piercing blade. Mercutio, hot with rage, met Tybalt point to point. Belligerently, he pushed aside a deadly blow. With the other, Mercutio attacked Tybalt, who ably fought back. Romeo shouted, "Stop, friends! Separate!" He pushed down their sword tips and rushed between Tybalt and Mercutio. Tybalt thrust under Romeo's arm and slew Mercutio. Then Tybalt ran. Romeo returned to the scene and avenged Mercutio's death with lightning strokes. Before I could separate the two, Romeo killed Tybalt. As Tybalt fell, Romeo ran. This is the truth, I swear on pain of death.

ACT III

TRANSLATION

CAPULET'S WIFE   He is a kinsman to the Montague;
Affection makes him false, he speaks not true.   175
Some twenty of them fought in this black strife,
And all those twenty could but kill one life.
I beg for justice, which thou, Prince, must give.
Romeo slew Tybalt; Romeo must not live.

PRINCE   Romeo slew him; he slew Mercutio   180
Who now the price of his dear blood doth owe?

MONTAGUE   Not Romeo, Prince; he was Mercutio's friend;
His fault concludes but what the law should end,
The life of Tybalt.

PRINCE   And for that offense
Immediately we do exile him hence.   185
I have an interest in your hate's proceeding,
My blood for your rude brawls doth lie a-bleeding;
But I'll amerce you with so strong a fine
That you shall all repent the loss of mine.
I will be deaf to pleading and excuses;   190
Nor tears, nor prayers shall purchase out abuses.
Therefore use none. Let Romeo hence in haste,
Else, when he is found, that hour is his last.
Bear hence this body, and attend our will.
Mercy but murders. pardoning those that kill.   195
[Exit, with others]

ORIGINAL

CAPULET'S WIFE Benvolio is a member of the Montague family. Bias makes him lie. There were twenty involved in this brawl and all of them killed only one man. I demand justice, Prince Escalus. Romeo killed Tybalt; Romeo must die for the crime.

PRINCE Romeo killed Tybalt, a Capulet; Tybalt killed Mercutio, a Montague. Why should one man be executed?

MONTAGUE Don't execute Romeo, Prince Escalus. He was Mercutio's friend. His crime brings the fight to an end by the death of Tybalt, who started the brawl.

PRINCE For killing Tybalt, I banish Romeo from Verona. I have some stake in this feud in that Mercutio was my relative. But I will charge you so large a fine that you will all regret my loss of a kinsman. I will hear no appeals or excuses. Neither tears nor prayers will buy pardon for lawbreakers. Don't beg. Let Romeo flee quickly. If he is discovered in Verona, he will die. Remove Tybalt's body and carry out my orders. Mercy encourages murder by pardoning killers. *[Exit, with others]*

ACT III

ACT III, SCENE 2

The same. Capulet's orchard.

[Enter JULIET alone]

JULIET   Gallop apace, you fiery-footed steeds,
Towards Phoebus' lodging! Such a wagoner
As Phaeton would whip you to the west
And bring in cloudy night immediately.
Spread thy close curtain, love-performing night,   5
That runaways' eyes may wink, and Romeo
Leap to these arms untalked of and unseen.
Lovers can see to do their amorous rites
By their own beauties; or, if love be blind,
It best agrees with night. Come, civil night,   10
Thou sober-suited matron, all in black,
And learn me how to lose a winning match,
Played for a pair of stainless maidenhoods.
Hood my unmanned blood, bating in my cheeks,
With thy black mantle till strange love grow bold,   15
Think true love acted simple modesty.
Come, night; come, Romeo; come, thou day in night;
For thou wilt lie upon the wings of night
Whiter than new snow upon a raven's back.
Come, gentle night; come, loving, black-browed night,   20
Give me my Romeo; and, when he shall die,
Take him and cut him out in little stars,
And he will make the face of heaven so fine
That all the world will be in love with night
And pay no worship to the garish sun.   25
O, I have bought the mansion of a love,
But not possessed it; and though I am sold,
Not yet enjoyed. So tedious is this day
As is the night before some festival
To an impatient child that hath new robes   30
And may not wear them. O, here comes my nurse,
[Enter NURSE, with cords]
And she brings news; and every tongue that speaks
But Romeo's name speaks heavenly eloquence.
Now, nurse, what news? What hast thou there?
The cords that Romeo bid thee fetch?

ACT III, SCENE 2

That same afternoon in Capulet's orchard.

[Enter JULIET alone]

JULIET

Hurry on, the horses that pull the sun across the sky. A driver like Phaeton could instantly drive you west and usher in the night. Night, close your curtains and encourage love. Let Romeo leap into my arms in secret. Lovers see well enough for romance. If love is blind, it is best suited for night. Come sober night and teach me to surrender my virginity to my husband. Conceal my inexperience. Cloak in black my blushing cheeks until I can overcome modesty and boldly perform loving acts. Come, night; come, Romeo. Illuminate our wedding night like snow on a raven's back. Come, gentle night; come, night of love. Give me my Romeo. And when he dies, cut him into little stars. Let him brighten the sky so all the world will love night and stop admiring the sun. Oh, I have bought the house of marriage, but have not moved in. I am committed to a husband, but he has not enjoyed me. This day drags like the hours preceding a festival. I feel like a fretful child who has new clothes but who can't wear them. Oh, here comes my nurse. *[The NURSE enters with the rope ladder]* And she brings news. Every person who pronounces Romeo's name speaks eloquently. Nurse, what news do you bring? What are you carrying. Is that the rope ladder that Romeo had you bring?

NURSE	Ay, ay, the cords. 35
	[Throws them down]
JULIET	Ay me! what news? Why dost thou wring thy hands?
NURSE	Ah, weraday! he's dead, he's dead, he's dead! We are undone, lady, we are undone! Alack the day! he's gone, he's killed, he's dead!
JULIET	Can heaven be so envious?
NURSE	Romeo can, 40 Though heaven cannot. O Romeo, Romeo! Who ever would have thought it? Romeo!
JULIET	What devil art thou that dost torment me thus? This torture should be roared in dismal hell. Hath Romeo slain himself? Say thou but 'I,' 45 And that bare vowel 'I' shall poison more Than the death-darting eye of cockatrice. I am not I, if there be such an 'I' Or those eyes shut that makes the answer 'I.' If he be slain, say 'I'; or if not, 'no.' 50 Brief sounds determine of my weal or woe.
NURSE	I saw the wound, I saw it with mine eyes, (God save the mark!) here on his manly breast. A piteous corse, a bloody piteous corse; Pale, pale as ashes, all bedaubed in blood, 55 All in gore-blood. I swounded at the sight.
JULIET	O, break, my heart! poor bankrupt, break at once! To prison, eyes; ne'er look on liberty! Vile earth, to earth resign; end motion here, And thou and Romeo press one heavy bier! 60
NURSE	O Tybalt, Tybalt, the best friend I had! O courteous Tybalt! honest gentleman! That ever I should live to see thee dead!
JULIET	What storm is this that blows so contrary? Is Romeo slaught'red, and is Tybalt dead? 65 My dearest cousin, and my dearer lord? Then, dreadful trumpet, sound the general doom! For who is living, if those two are gone?
NURSE	Tybalt is gone, and Romeo banished; Romeo that killed him, he is banished; 70

ORIGINAL

NURSE	Yes, yes, the rope ladder. *[Throws them down]*
JULIET	Oh me! What news do you bring? Why are you wringing your hands?
NURSE	Oh, terrible news! He's dead. We are ruined, lady, we are ruined! Terrible day—he's been murdered.
JULIET	Can heaven begrudge me happiness?
NURSE	Romeo can begrudge it. Oh Romeo! Who could have imagined it? Romeo!
JULIET	Why do you torture me? Are you a demon? This torment belongs in hell. Has Romeo killed himself? Say only "Yes" and you release more poison than a fabled serpent. If you say yes, I will not survive. Are Romeo's eyes closed forever? Say yes or no. One word shall determine my future.
NURSE	I saw the wound with my own eyes (God pardon me) here on his chest. His corpse was pitiful and bloody—pale as ashes, spotted with blood and clots. I fainted at the sight.
JULIET	Oh, break, my heart! Empty of love, break at once! Eyes, never look on freedom again. Vile body, give yourself to the grave. Stop moving. Join Romeo in his coffin!
NURSE	Oh Tybalt, my best friend. Oh courteous Tybalt, a respectable gentleman! I never expected to see you dead!
JULIET	Why do you change the subject? Is Romeo murdered and Tybalt also dead? My dearest cousin Tybalt and my husband Romeo? Doom has fallen! Why go on living if those two are gone?
NURSE	Tybalt is dead and Romeo banished. For killing Tybalt, Romeo is in exile.

ACT III

TRANSLATION

JULIET	O God! Did Romeo's hand shed Tybalt's blood?
NURSE	It did, it did! alas the day, it did!
JULIET	O serpent heart, hid with a flow'ring face!
	Did ever dragon keep so fair a cave?
	Beautiful tyrant! fiend angelical! 75
	Dove-feathered raven! wolvish-ravening lamb!
	Despised substance of divinest show!
	Just opposite to what thou justly seem'st—
	A damned saint, an honorable villain!
	O nature, what hadst thou to do in hell 80
	When thou didst bower the spirit of a fiend
	In mortal paradise of such sweet flesh?
	Was ever book containing such vile matter
	So fairly bound? O, that deceit should dwell
	In such a gorgeous palace!
NURSE	There's no trust, 85
	No faith, no honesty in men; all perjured,
	All forsworn, all naught, all dissemblers.
	Ah, where's my man? Give me some aqua vitae.
	These griefs, these woes, these sorrows make me old.
	Shame come to Romeo!
JULIET	Blistered be thy tongue 90
	For such a wish! He was not born to shame.
	Upon his brow shame is ashamed to sit;
	For 'tis a throne where honor may be crowned
	Sole monarch of the universal earth.
	O, what a beast was I to chide at him! 95
NURSE	Will you speak well of him that killed your cousin?
JULIET	Shall I speak ill of him that is my husband?
	Ah, poor my lord, what tongue shall smooth thy name
	When I, thy three-hours wife, have mangled it?
	But wherefore, villain, didst thou kill my cousin? 100
	That villain cousin would have killed my husband.
	Back, foolish tears, back to your native spring!
	Your tributary drops belong to woe,
	Which you, mistaking, offer up to joy.
	My husband lives, that Tybalt would have slain; 105
	And Tybalt's dead, that would have slain my husband.
	All this is comfort; wherefore weep I then?
	Some word there was, worser than Tybalt's death,
	That murd'red me. I would forget it fain;
	But O, it presses to my memory 110
	Like damned guilty deeds to sinners' minds!

ORIGINAL

JULIET	Oh God! Did Romeo kill Tybalt?
NURSE	He did, he did! Alas, he did!
JULIET	Oh evil heart beating in a handsome body! Did a dragon ever live in so attractive a cave? Beautiful killer! Angelic demon! Oh raven in dove's feather! Oh lamb that attacks wolves! A despised man with divine looks! You are the opposite of what you seem to be—a cursed saint, a respectable criminal! Oh nature, how could you combine a demon's spirit in such a sweet person? Was there ever so despised a book so beautifully bound? Oh, how could deceit live in so gorgeous a body!
NURSE	Men are not trustworthy, faithful, or honest. All lie and cheat. Oh, where's my servant! Give me some restorative drink. These griefs and sorrows age me. Shame on Romeo!
JULIET	Blisters on your tongue for shaming Romeo. He is not worthy of shame. Shame doesn't belong on his face. Honor should reside there. Oh, I was beastly to defame him!
NURSE	Will you defend the man who killed your cousin Tybalt?
JULIET	Should I defame my own husband? Oh, poor Romeo, who will defend you when your own wife of three hours has defamed you? Why did you kill my cousin? That wicked cousin would have killed my husband. Tears belong to sorrow. I mistakenly shed them for happiness that Romeo was not killed. Romeo survived Tybalt's attack; Tybalt died instead. There is comfort in that thought. Why am I crying? There was something else worse than Tybalt's death. I would quickly forget it, but it refuses to leave my memory.

ACT III

TRANSLATION

'Tybalt is dead, and Romeo—banished.'
That 'banished,' that one word 'banished,'
Hath slain ten thousand Tybalts. Tybalt's death
Was woe enough, if it had ended there;   115
Or, if sour woe delights in fellowship
And needly will be ranked with other griefs,
Why followed not, when she said 'Tybalt's dead,'
Thy father, or thy mother, nay, or both,
Which modern lamentation might have moved?   120
But with a rearward following Tybalt's death,
'Romeo is banished'—to speak that word
Is father, mother, Tybalt, Romeo, Juliet,
All slain, all dead. 'Romeo is banished'—
There is no end, no limit, measure, bound,   125
In that word's death; no words can that woe sound.
Where is my father and my mother, nurse?

NURSE   Weeping and wailing over Tybalt's corse.
Will you go to them? I will bring you thither.

JULIET   Wash they his wounds with tears? Mine shall be spent,   130
When theirs are dry, for Romeo's banishment.
Take up those cords. Poor ropes, you are beguiled,
Both you and I, for Romeo is exiled.
He made you for a highway to my bed;
But I a maid, die maiden-widowed.   135
Come, cords; come, nurse I'll to my wedding bed;
And death, not Romeo, take my maidenhead!

NURSE   Hie to your chamber. I'll find Romeo
To comfort you. I wot well where he is.
Hark ye, your Romeo will be here at night.   140
I'll to him; he is hid at Laurence' cell.

JULIET   O, find him! give this ring to my true knight
And bid him come to take his last farewell.
[Exit with NURSE]

ORIGINAL

Tybalt is dead; Romeo is banished. The word "banished" is more woeful than the death of ten thousand Tybalts. Tybalt's death was sad enough, if that were all of the bad news. If I needed some other sorrow to mourn, why didn't the nurse say that Tybalt and my father or my mother or both parents had died? By adding to Tybalt's death Romeo's exile—it is as bad as the killing of my parents, Romeo, and me. "Banished" is as woeful a word as "dead." Where are my father and mother, nurse?

NURSE	They are weeping over Tybalt's corpse. Are you going to join them? I will escort you.
JULIET	Are they washing his wounds with tears? I will weep for Romeo's exile. Take back the rope ladder. Poor cords, you and I are cheated. Romeo is banished. Romeo made this ladder as an access to my bed. I will die a widowed virgin. Come, rope, come nurse. I will die in my bed a virgin.
NURSE	Hurry to your room. I'll find Romeo to comfort you. I know where he is. Romeo will come here tonight. I'll find him in his hiding place, Friar Laurence's room.
JULIET	Oh, find him! Give him this ring and have him come to me to say goodbye. *[JULIET goes out with the NURSE]*

ACT III

TRANSLATION

ACT III, SCENE 3

The same. Friar Laurence's cell.

[Enter FRIAR LAURENCE]

FRIAR	Romeo, come forth; come forth, thou fearful man.
	Affliction is enamored of thy parts,
	And thou art wedded to calamity.
	[Enter ROMEO]

ROMEO Father, what news? What is the Prince's doom?
What sorrow craves acquaintance at my hand   5
That I yet know not?

FRIAR   Too familiar
Is my dear son with such sour company.
I bring thee tidings of the Prince's doom.

ROMEO What less than doomsday is the Prince's doom?

FRIAR A gentler judgment vanished from his lips—   10
Not body's death, but body's banishment.

ROMEO Ha, banishment? Be merciful, say 'death';
For exile hath more terror in his look,
Much more than death. Do not say 'banishment.'

FRIAR Hence from Verona art thou banished.   15
Be patient, for the world is broad and wide.

ROMEO There is no world without Verona walls,
But purgatory, torture, hell itself.
Hence banished is banished from the world,
And world's exile is death. Then 'banished'   20
Is death mistermed. Calling death 'banished"
Thou cut'st my head off with a golden axe
And smilest upon the stroke that murders me.

FRIAR O deadly sin! O rude unthankfulness!
Thy fault our law calls death; but the kind Prince,   25
Taking thy part, hath rushed aside the law,
And turned that black word 'death' to banishment.
This is dear mercy, and thou seest it not.

ACT III, SCENE 3

The same afternoon in Friar Laurence's room.

[FRIAR LAURENCE enters]

FRIAR	Romeo, come out of hiding. You are perpetually troubled and headed for disaster. *[Enter ROMEO]*
ROMEO	Father Laurence, what is Prince Escalus's sentence? What punishment awaits me?
FRIAR	You are too often weighted down with gloom. I bring news of the prince's judgment.
ROMEO	Is his sentence any less than the end of the world?
FRIAR	A better sentence—he demands your exile, not your execution.
ROMEO	I am banished? A death sentence would be more merciful. Exile is worse than death. Don't say "banishment."
FRIAR	You must leave Verona. Be resigned. The world is a big place.
ROMEO	There is nothing outside Verona but torment and hell. Exile means I am banished from my world. Exile is the same as death. By banishing me, the prince smiles as he decapitates me with a golden axe.
FRIAR	You are guilty of a deadly sin—you show no gratitude. The kind prince, on your behalf, has abandoned capital punishment and let you live in exile. You don't see that this is an act of mercy.

ACT III

TRANSLATION

ROMEO	'Tis torture, and not mercy. Heaven is here,
	Where Juliet lives; and every cat and dog 30
	And little mouse, every unworthy thing,
	Live here in heaven and may look on her;
	But Romeo may not. More validity,
	More honorable state, more courtship lives
	In carrion flies than Romeo. They may seize 35
	On the white wonder of dear Juliet's hand
	And steal immortal blessing from her lips,
	Who, even in pure and vestal modesty,
	Still blush, as thinking their own kisses sin;
	But Romeo may not, he is banished. 40
	Flies may do this but I from this must fly;
	They are freemen, but I am banished.
	And sayest thou yet that exile is not death?
	Hadst thou no poison mixed, no sharp-ground knife,
	No sudden mean of death, though ne'er so mean 45
	But 'banished' to kill me—'banished'?
	O friar, the damned use that word in hell;
	Howling attends it! How hast thou the heart,
	Being a divine, a ghostly confessor,
	A sin-absolver, and my friend professed, 50
	To mangle me with that word 'banished'?
FRIAR	Thou fond mad man, hear me a little speak.
ROMEO	O, thou wilt speak again of banishment.
FRIAR	I'll give thee armor to keep off that word;
	Adversity's sweet milk, philosophy, 55
	To comfort thee, though thou art banished.
ROMEO	Yet 'banished'? Hang up philosophy!
	Unless philosophy can make a Juliet,
	Displant a town, reverse a prince's doom,
	It helps not, it prevails not. Talk no more. 60
FRIAR	O, then I see that madmen have no ears.
ROMEO	How should they, when that wise men have no eyes?
FRIAR	Let me dispute with thee of thy estate.

ORIGINAL

ROMEO	Exile is torture, not mercy. Heaven is here where Juliet lives. Every cat, dog, and mouse can enjoy her company, but I can't. Even flies enjoy more respect in touching her than I. Even insects can admire Juliet's hand and be blessed by her lips. She is so modest that she blushes when she kisses me. Romeo has less access to Juliet than do flies. Insects are free, but I am exiled. And you demand that I should not feel sad that I am banished? Have you no poison, sharp knife, no other weapon to kill me other than exile? Oh Friar Laurence, the damned are banished to hell. They howl at the word "exile"! Do you have the heart to assault me with exile, you, my spiritual counselor and friend?

FRIAR	You silly madman, listen to me.
ROMEO	Don't mention exile again.
FRIAR	I will strengthen you with counsel. I will comfort you, even though you are banished.
ROMEO	Sent away forever? Forget good advice! Unless counsel can supply me Juliet and reverse the prince's judgment, your words give me no comfort. Don't say anything else.
FRIAR	I realize that frenzied men don't listen.
ROMEO	Why should they listen when counselors don't recognize misery?
FRIAR	Let me discuss with you your position.

TRANSLATION

ROMEO	Thou canst not speak of that thou dost not feel.
	Wert thou as young as I, Juliet thy love, 65
	An hour but married, Tybalt murdered,
	Doting like me, and like me banished,
	Then mightst thou speak, then mightst thou tear thy hair,
	And fall upon the ground, as I do now,
	Taking the measure of an unmade grave. 70
	[Enter NURSE and knocks]
FRIAR	Arise; one knocks. Good Romeo, hide thyself.
ROMEO	Not I: unless the breath of heartsick groans
	Mist-like infold me from the search of eyes. *[Knock]*
FRIAR	Hark, how they knock! Who's there? Romeo, arise;
	Thou wilt be taken.—Stay awhile!—Stand up; 75
	[Knock]
	Run to my study.—By and by!—God's will,
	What simpleness is this.—I come, I come! *[Knock]*
	Who knocks so hard? Whence come you? What's your will?
	[Enter NURSE]
NURSE	Let me come in, and you shall know my errand.
	I come from Lady Juliet.
FRIAR	Welcome then. 80
NURSE	O holy friar, O, tell me, holy friar,
	Where is my lady's lord, where's Romeo?
FRIAR	There on the ground, with his own tears made drunk.
NURSE	O, he is even in my mistress' case,
	Just in her case! O woeful sympathy! 85
	Piteous predicament! Even so lies she,
	Blubb'ring and weeping, weeping and blubb'ring.
	Stand up, stand up! Stand, an you be a man.
	For Juliet's sake, for her sake, rise and stand!
	Why should you fall into so deep an O? 90
ROMEO	*[Rises]* Nurse—
NURSE	Ah sir! ah sir! Death's the end of all.
ROMEO	Spakest thou of Juliet? How is it with her?
	Doth not she think me an old murderer,
	Now I have stained the childhood of our joy 95
	With blood removed but little from her own?
	Where is she? and how doth she! and what says
	My concealed lady to our cancelled love?

ORIGINAL

ROMEO	You can't discuss something that has never happened to you. If you were young and Juliet were your bride; if Tybalt were killed and you yourself exiled, then you could say something meaningful. You could tear your hair and fall on the ground as though readying yourself for the grave. *[Enter NURSE and knocks]*
FRIAR	Get up. Someone is at the door. Hide.
ROMEO	I won't hide unless my groans wrap me in mist. *[Knock]*
FRIAR	Listen to the knocking! *[To the newcomer]* Who's there? *[To Romeo]* Romeo, get up. You will be arrested. *[To the newcomer]* I'm coming! *[To Romeo]* Stand up. *[Knock]* Run to my office. *[To the newcomer]* I will be with you shortly. *[To Romeo]* How foolishly you are behaving. *[To the newcomer]* I'm coming. *[Knock]* Who knocks so loud? Where did you come from? What do you want? *[Enter NURSE]*
NURSE	Let me in and I'll tell you. I come from Juliet.
FRIAR	Then you are welcome.
NURSE	Oh holy friar, Oh, tell me, holy friar, where is Juliet's husband? Where's Romeo?
FRIAR	There on the ground soaked in tears.
NURSE	Oh, he is behaving like Juliet. Just like her! Oh sad spectacle, a pitiful dilemma! Juliet also lies blubbering and sobbing, sobbing and blubbering. Get up! Stand if you are a man. For Juliet's sake, get up! Why do you mourn so deeply?
ROMEO	*[Rises]* Nurse —
NURSE	Ah sir! Everyone dies in the end.
ROMEO	Are you talking about Juliet? Is she all right? Does she think of me as a killer, now that I have slain her cousin? Where is Juliet? How is she? What does my new wife think of our ruined marriage?

ACT III

TRANSLATION

NURSE	O, she says nothing, sir, but weeps and weeps;
	And now falls on her bed, and then starts up,	100
	And Tybalt calls; and then on Romeo cries,
	And then down falls again.

ROMEO	As if that name,
	Shot from the deadly level of a gun,
	Did murder her; as that name's cursed hand
	Murdered her kinsman. O, tell me, friar, tell me,	105
	In what vile part of this anatomy
	Doth my name lodge? Tell me, that I may sack
	The hateful mansion.
	[He offers to stab himself, and Nurse snatches
	the dagger away]

FRIAR	Hold thy desperate hand.
	Art thou a man? Thy form cries out thou art;
	Thy tears are womanish, thy wild acts denote	110
	The unreasonable fury of a beast.
	Unseemly woman in a seeming man!
	And ill-beseeming beast in seeming both!
	Thou hast amazed me. By my holy order,
	I thought thy disposition better tempered.	115
	Hast thou slain Tybalt? Wilt thou slay thyself?
	And slay thy lady that in thy life lives,
	By doing damned hate upon thyself?
	Why railest thou on thy birth, the heaven, and earth?
	Since birth and heaven and earth, all three do meet	120
	In thee at once; which thou at once wouldst lose.
	Fie, fie, thou shamest thy shape, thy love, thy wit,
	Which, like a usurer, abound'st in all,
	And usest none in that true use indeed
	Which should bedeck thy shape, thy love, thy wit.	125
	Thy noble shape is but a form of wax,
	Digressing from the valor of a man;
	Thy dear love sworn but hollow perjury,
	Killing that love which thou hast vowed to cherish;
	Thy wit, that ornament to shape and love,	130
	Misshapen in the conduct of them both,
	Like powder in a skilless soldier's flask,
	Is set afire by thine own ignorance,
	And thou dismemb'red with thine own defense.
	What, rouse thee, man! Thy Juliet is alive,	135
	For whose dear sake thou wast but lately dead.
	There art thou happy. Tybalt would kill thee,
	But thou slewest Tybalt. There art thou happy too.
	The law, that threat'ned death, becomes thy friend

ORIGINAL

NURSE   She says nothing, but she sobs and sobs. She collapses on
                 her bed, then gets up and cries out for Tybalt. Then she
                 cries for Romeo and collapses again.

ROMEO   As if I had murdered her. My name is charged with
                 Tybalt's slaying. Oh, tell me, Friar Laurence. In what part
                 of my body does my name live? Tell me where so I can
                 cut it out with my dagger. *[He tries to stab himself.
                 The nurse snatches away the dagger]*

FRIAR   Stop trying to kill yourself. Act like an adult. You look
                 like a man, but your weeping is womanish. Your despera-
                 tion resembles the rage of a beast. You look like a man,
                 but act like a woman. By being both mannish and wom-
                 anish, you are a strange beast. You shock me. By my holy
                 calling, I thought you better behaved than this. Did you
                 kill Tybalt? Will you commit suicide? Will you kill your
                 wife by destroying yourself? Why do you rant about your
                 life, heaven, and earth? When you were born, heaven
                 and earth worked together to make you. You would give
                 up all three with one thrust of your dagger. Shame,
                 shame, you dishonor your body, your marriage, your
                 intellect, the characteristics that live in you. You betray
                 yourself with thoughts of suicide. Your handsome body is
                 no more durable than wax if you abandon your sense.
                 You lie if you betray your marriage vows and if you kill
                 the bride whom you promised to cherish. Your reason
                 fails both your manhood and your marriage, like gun-
                 powder that the inexperienced soldier accidentally
                 ignites. The clumsy act destroys you rather than defends
                 you. Get up, Romeo! Your wife is alive, for whose sake
                 you were willing to die. You are a lucky man. You killed
                 Tybalt before he could kill you. That is good fortune.
                 The law could have demanded your execution.

TRANSLATION

And turns it to exile. There art thou happy. 140
A pack of blessings light upon thy back;
Happiness courts thee in her best array;
But, like a misbehaved and sullen wench,
Thou pout'st upon thy fortune and thy love.
Take heed, take heed, for such die miserable. 145
Go get thee to thy love, as was decreed,
Ascend her chamber, hence and comfort her.
But look thou stay not till the watch be set,
For then thou canst not pass to Mantua,
Where thou shalt live till we can find a time 150
To blaze your marriage, reconcile your friends,
Beg pardon of the Prince, and call thee back
With twenty hundred thousand times more joy
Than thou went'st forth in lamentation.
Go before, nurse. Commend me to thy lady, 155
And bid her hasten all the house to bed,
Which heavy sorrow makes them apt unto.
Romeo is coming.

NURSE   O Lord, I could have stayed here all the night
To hear good counsel. O, what learning is! 160
My lord, I'll tell my lady you will come.

ROMEO   Do so, and bid my sweet prepare to chide.

NURSE   Here is a ring she bid me give you, sir.
Hie you, make haste, for it grows very late. *[Exit]*

ROMEO   How well my comfort is revived by this! 165

FRIAR   Go hence; good night; and here stands all your state:
Either be gone before the watch be set,
Or by the break of day disguised from hence.
Sojourn in Mantua. I'll find out your man,
And he shall signify from time to time 170
Every good hap to you that chances here.
Give me thy hand. 'Tis late. Farewell; good night.

ROMEO   But that a joy past joy calls out on me,
It were a grief so brief to part with thee.
Farewell. *[Exeunt]* 175

ORIGINAL

You are again lucky in being banished rather than executed. Blessings surround you. Fortune favors you. But you are behaving like a pouty girl who misbehaves and complains about her fate. Be warned that such people die miserably. Hurry to Juliet. Climb the ladder to her room and comfort her. Don't stay too long, because Mantua has a curfew. You must live there until we can arrange a wedding announcement. We will satisfy your friends with the news and seek a pardon from Prince Escalus. Then you may return to Verona with twenty hundred thousand times more joy than the grief you bore when you left. Leave now, nurse, and give my message to Juliet. Have her send the Capulets to bed to rest from their mourning. Romeo is on the way.

NURSE	Oh Lord, I would have spent the night here in anticipation of good advice. Oh, how valuable is education. Romeo, I will tell Juliet that you will come to her.
ROMEO	Tell her and ask her to be ready to scold me.
NURSE	Here is a ring she sent to you. Hurry. It's getting late. *[She departs]*
ROMEO	This visit has lifted my spirits!
FRIAR	Go to Juliet. Good night. Your safety depends on timing: Either leave before the night watch begins or else disguise yourself and slip out at daybreak. Stay in Mantua. I'll question your servant from time to time about your chances of returning from exile to Verona. Give me your hand. It is late. Farewell. Good night.
ROMEO	Unparalleled joy summons me. Otherwise, I would be sorry to leave you so abruptly. Farewell. *[They go out]*

TRANSLATION

ACT III, SCENE 4

The same. A room in Capulet's house.

[Enter old CAPULET, his WIFE, and PARIS]

CAPULET	Things have fall'n out, sir, so unluckily	
	That we have had no time to move our daughter.	
	Look you, she loved her kinsman Tybalt dearly,	
	And so did I. Well, we were born to die.	
	'Tis very late; she'll not come down to-night.	5
	I promise you, but for your company,	
	I would have been abed an hour ago.	
PARIS	These times of woe afford no times to woo.	
	Madam, good night. Commend me to your daughter.	
LADY	I will, and know her mind early to-morrow;	10
	To-night she's mewed up to her heaviness.	
CAPULET	Sir Paris, I will make a desperate tender	
	Of my child's love. I think she will be ruled	
	In all respects by me; nay more, I doubt it not.	
	Wife, go you to her ere you go to bed;	15
	Acquaint her here of my son Paris' love	
	And bid her (mark you me?) on Wednesday next—	
	But soft! what day is this?	
PARIS	Monday, my lord.	
CAPULET	Monday! ha, ha! Well, Wednesday is too soon.	
	A Thursday let it be—a Thursday, tell her,	20
	She shall be married to this noble earl.	
	Will you be ready? Do you like this haste?	
	We'll keep no great ado—a friend or two;	
	For hark you, Tybalt being slain so late,	
	It may be thought we held him carelessly,	25
	Being our kinsman, if we revel much.	
	Therefore we'll have some half a dozen friends,	
	And there an end. But what say you to Thursday?	

ACT III, SCENE 4

The same evening. A room in Capulet's house.

[Enter old CAPULET, his WIFE, and PARIS]

CAPULET   Misfortunes have occurred, Count Paris, that leave us no time to persuade Juliet to marry you. You see, she loved her cousin Tybalt dearly, and so did I. Well, everyone must die sometime. It is late. She has already gone to bed. If you weren't visiting, I would have gone to bed an hour ago.

PARIS   In times of sorrow, there is no opportunity for courtship. Madam, good night. Give my regards to Juliet.

LADY   I will and I will ask her tomorrow about your marriage proposal. Tonight she is shut in her room in mourning.

CAPULET   Paris, I will try to persuade her to accept. I think she will follow her father's wishes. There is no doubt, I'm sure she will. Wife, visit Juliet before you go to bed. Tell her of Paris's love for her. Tell her (are you listening?) that on next Wednesday . . . . Wait, what day is this?

PARIS   Monday, my lord.

CAPULET   Monday is it? Well Wednesday is too soon. Let's settle on Thursday. Tell her that, on Thursday, she will marry noble Paris. Will you be ready, Paris? Is this not too hasty for you? We'll keep the wedding simple—a friend or two as witnesses. Because Tybalt was killed today, people may think we are dishonoring his memory if we celebrate too much at a wedding. Therefore, we will invite a half dozen friends and no more. What do you think of Thursday as a wedding date?

TRANSLATION

PARIS	My lord, I would that Thursday were tomorrow.
CAPULET	Well, get you gone. A Thursday be it then. 30
	Go you to Juliet ere you go to bed;
	Prepare her, wife, against this wedding day.
	Farewell, my lord.—Light to my chamber, ho!
	Afore me, it is so very very late
	That we may call it early by and by. 35
	Good night.
	[Exeunt]

PARIS My lord, I wish it were already Thursday.

CAPULET Well, that's enough for tonight. Next Thursday will be the wedding. Wife, visit Juliet before you go to bed. Prepare her for marriage. Farewell, Paris. *[To a servant]* Light my way to the bedroom. It is so late that it is almost morning. Good night. *[The Capulets depart]*

TRANSLATION

ACT III, SCENE 5

The same. Juliet's chamber.

[Enter ROMEO and JULIET aloft, at the window]

JULIET	Wilt thou be gone? It is not yet near day.
	It was the nightingale, and not the lark,
	That pierced the fearful hollow of thine ear.
	Nightly she sings on yond pomegranate tree.
	Believe me, love, it was the nightingale. 5
ROMEO	It was the lark, the herald of the morn;
	No nightingale. Look, love, what envious streaks
	Do lace the severing clouds in yonder East.
	Night's candles are burnt out, and jocund day
	Stands tiptoe on the misty mountain tops. 10
	I must be gone and live, or stay and die.
JULIET	Yond light is not daylight; I know it, I.
	It is some meteor that the sun exhales
	To be to thee this night a torchbearer
	And light thee on thy way to Mantua. 15
	Therefore stay yet; thou need'st not to be gone.
ROMEO	Let me be ta'en, let me be put to death.
	I am content, so thou wilt have it so.
	I'll say yon grey is not the morning's eye,
	'Tis but the pale reflex of Cynthia's brow; 20
	Nor that is not the lark whose notes do beat
	The vaulty heaven so high above our heads.
	I have more care to stay than will to go.
	Come, death, and welcome! Juliet wills it so.
	How is't, my soul? Let's talk; it is not day. 25
JULIET	It is, it is! Hie hence, be gone, away!
	It is the lark that sings so out of tune,
	Straining harsh discords and unpleasing sharps.
	Some say the lark makes sweet division;
	This doth not so, for she divideth us. 30
	Some say the lark and loathed toad change eyes;
	O, now I would they had changed voices too,
	Since arm from arm that voice doth us affray,
	Hunting thee hence with hunts-up to the day.
	O, now be gone! More light and light it grows. 35

ORIGINAL

ACT III, SCENE 5

That same night. Juliet's bedroom.

[JULIET stands at the window with ROMEO]

JULIET	Are you leaving? It isn't dawn yet. That was the nightingale, not the lark we heard. Every night she sings from the pomegranate tree. Believe me, love, it was a nightingale we heard.
ROMEO	It was a lark, which announces the morning. It wasn't a nightingale. Look, love, where sunrise streaks clouds to the east. The stars are gone and day appears at the mountain tops. I must be gone if I want to live. If I stay, I will be executed.
JULIET	It isn't daybreak. It is a meteor that lights your way to Mantua. Stay longer. You don't need to leave.
ROMEO	I wouldn't mind being arrested and executed if that is what you want. I'll say that the gray is not the emergence of morning but only a reflection of the moon. It is not the lark singing in the sky above. I prefer to stay. I welcome death. Juliet wants me to stay. What do you think, my soul? Let's talk. It isn't morning.
JULIET	It is! Hurry away, go to Mantua! It is the lark singing harsh tunes. Some people say the lark sings sweetly. It isn't true. The lark is parting us. Some say the lark swapped eyes with the toad. I wish the lark and toad had swapped voices, since the song is separating us. The lark's song calls you like the hunter's signal. Oh, hurry! The sky is getting lighter.

ACT III

TRANSLATION

ROMEO	More light and light—more dark and dark our woes. *[Enter NURSE, hastily]*
NURSE	Madam!
JULIET	Nurse?
NURSE	Your lady mother is coming to your chamber. The day is broke; be wary, look about. *[Exit]*
JULIET	Then, window, let day in, and let life out.
ROMEO	Farewell, farewell! One kiss, and I'll descend. *[He goeth down]*
JULIET	Art thou gone so, love-lord, ay husband-friend? I must hear from thee every day in the hour, For in a minute there are many days. O, by this count I shall be much in years Ere I again behold my Romeo!
ROMEO	Farewell! I will omit no opportunity That may convey my greetings, love, to thee.
JULIET	O, think'st thou we shall ever meet again?
ROMEO	I doubt it not; and all these woes shall serve For sweet discourses in our times to come.
JULIET	O God, I have an ill-divining soul! Methinks I see thee, now thou art so low, As one dead in the bottom of a tomb. Either my eyesight fails, or thou lookest pale.
ROMEO	And trust me, love, in my eye so do you. Dry sorrow drinks our blood. Adieu, adieu! *[Exit]*
JULIET	O Fortune, Fortune! all men call thee fickle. If thou art fickle, what dost thou with him That is renowned for faith? Be fickle, Fortune, For then I hope thou wilt not keep him long But send him back. *[She goeth down from the window. Enter Mother]*
LADY	Ho, daughter! are you up?
JULIET	Who is't that calls? It is my lady mother. Is she not down so late, or up so early? What unaccustomed cause procures her hither?

Line numbers: 40, 45, 50, 55, 60, 65

ORIGINAL

ROMEO   The brighter the day is, the darker our spirits become.
[Enter NURSE, hastily]

NURSE   Madam!

JULIET   Nurse?

NURSE   Your mother is coming to your room. It is daybreak.
Be cautious. *[The NURSE goes out]*

JULIET   Then, window, let in daylight and let my beloved depart.

ROMEO   Farewell, farewell! One kiss and I will climb down.
[He climbs down the rope ladder]

JULIET   Are you gone, lover, husband, and friend? I must hear
from you every hour of the day. Even a minute apart
seems like days. By this way of counting time, I will be an
old woman before I see my Romeo again.

ROMEO   Farewell! I will take every opportunity to send messages
to you, Juliet.

JULIET   Do you think we will ever meet again?

ROMEO   Certainly we will meet again. Then we will discuss for
years to come the desperation of our wedding day.

JULIET   Oh God, I sense ill omens! When I look down on you, I
see you buried in a grave. Either my eyes are failing or
you are pale.

ROMEO   Believe me, love, you also look pale to me. Sorrow makes
us pale. Goodbye, goodbye! *[He goes out]*

JULIET   Oh luck! everyone says you are unpredictable. If you are
unreliable, how do you treat the faithful? Be changeable,
luck, by not keeping Romeo away too long and by send-
ing him back to me. *[She goes down from the window.
Enter Mother]*

LADY   Juliet, are you awake?

JULIET   Who is calling me? It is my mother. Why was she up so
late and arisen so early? What unusual errand brings
her here?

ACT III

TRANSLATION

LADY	Why, how now, Juliet?
JULIET	Madam, I am not well.

LADY Evermore weeping for your cousin's death?   70
What, wilt thou wash him from his grave with tears?
An if thou couldst, thou couldst not make him live.
Therefore have done. Some grief shows much of love;
But much of grief shows still some want of wit.

JULIET Yet let me weep for such a feeling loss.   75

LADY So shall you feel the loss, but not the friend
Which you weep for.

JULIET   Feeling so the loss,
I cannot choose but ever weep the friend.

LADY Well, girl, thou weep'st not so much for his death
As that the villain lives which slaughtered him.   80

JULIET What villain, madam?

LADY   That same villain Romeo.

JULIET [Aside] Villain and he be many miles asunder.—
God pardon him! I do, with all my heart;
And yet no man like he doth grieve my heart.

LADY That is because the traitor murderer lives.   85

JULIET Ay, madam, from the reach of these my hands.
Would none but I might venge my cousin's death!

LADY We will have vengeance for it, fear thou not.
Then weep no more. I'll send to one in Mantua,
Where that same banished runagate doth live,   90
Shall give him such an unaccustomed dram
That he shall soon keep Tybalt company;
And then I hope thou wilt be satisfied.

JULIET Indeed I never shall be satisfied
With Romeo till I behold him—dead—   95
Is my poor heart so for a kinsman vexed.
Madam, if you could find out but a man
To bear a poison, I would temper it;
That Romeo should, upon receipt thereof,
Soon sleep in quiet. O, how my heart abhors   100
To hear him named and cannot come to him,
To wreak the love I bore my cousin
Upon his body that hath slaughtered him!

ORIGINAL

LADY	Is that you, Juliet?
JULIET	Madam, I feel ill.
LADY	Are you still mourning Tybalt? Will you wash him out of the grave with tears? Even so, you couldn't bring him back to life. So stop crying. Sorrow is a sign of love, but too much sorrow makes you seem witless.
JULIET	Let me mourn for my loss.
LADY	You will always be sad for him, but he will not return.
JULIET	I am so sad that I must always mourn for him.
LADY	Well, Juliet, you aren't grieving for Tybalt as much as you mourn the fact that his killer is still alive.
JULIET	What criminal, madam?
LADY	The felon Romeo.
JULIET	*[To herself]* Romeo is a long way from being a criminal. *[To her mother]* May God pardon Romeo. I heartily pardon him, but he is not the reason for my grief.
LADY	You mourn because the killer is still alive.
JULIET	Yes, ma'am, he is far from me. Only I can avenge Tybalt's death!
LADY	The Capulets will have vengeance, don't you worry. Stop crying. I will hire someone in Mantua, where the exiled Romeo lives, and have the hireling poison Romeo. The killer will soon join Tybalt in death. Then you will be satisfied.
JULIET	I will never be satisfied until I see Romeo—dead. My heart is in turmoil for my cousin Tybalt. Madam, if you can locate a killer to get the poison, I will mix it. Then Romeo shall drink it and sleep forever. Oh, I detest his name. I can't kill the swordsman to avenge Tybalt.

ACT III

TRANSLATION

LADY	Find thou the means, and I'll find such a man. But now I'll tell thee joyful tidings, girl.	105
JULIET	And joy comes well in such a needy time. What are they, beseech your ladyship?	
LADY	Well, well, thou hast a careful father, child; One who, to put thee from thy heaviness, Hath sorted out a sudden day of joy That thou expects not nor I looked not for.	110
JULIET	Madam, in happy time! What day is that?	
LADY	Marry, my child, early next Thursday morn The gallant, young, and noble gentleman, The County Paris, at Saint Peter's Church, Shall happily make thee there a joyful bride.	115
JULIET	Now by Saint Peter's Church, and Peter, too, He shall not make me there a joyful bride! I wonder at this haste, that I must wed Ere he that should be husband comes to woo. I pray you tell my lord and father, madam, I will not marry yet; and when I do, I swear It shall be Romeo, whom you know I hate, Rather than Paris. These are news indeed!	120
LADY	Here comes your father. Tell him so yourself, And see how he will take it at your hands. *[Enter CAPULET and NURSE]*	125
CAPULET	When the sun sets the earth doth drizzle dew, But for the sunset of my brother's son It rains downright. How now? a conduit, girl? What, still in tears? Evermore show'ring? In one little body Thou counterfeit'st a bark, a sea, a wind: For still thy eyes, which I may call the sea, Do ebb and flow with tears; the bark thy body is, Sailing in this salt flood; the winds, thy sighs, Who, raging with thy tears and they with them, Without a sudden calm will overset Thy tempest-tossed body. How now, wife? Have you delivered to her our decree?	130 135
LADY	Ay, sir; but she will none, she gives you thanks. I would the fool were married to her grave!	140

LADY	You find the poison; I'll find a poisoner. I have joyful news for you, Juliet.
JULIET	I need some relief from sorrow. What is your news, your ladyship?
LADY	You have a dedicated father, child. To save you from sorrow, he has chosen a blessed day that you don't expect and I didn't foresee.
JULIET	Madam, what day is that?
LADY	On Thursday morning at Saint Peter's Church, Count Paris will marry you.
JULIET	I swear by the Church and by St. Peter that I won't marry Paris. This haste is inappropriate. He hasn't courted me. Please tell my father that I will not marry yet. When I do marry, it will be Romeo, whom the Capulets hate. I won't marry Paris. That is indeed news!
LADY	Here comes your father. Tell him so yourself and see how he reacts. *[Enter CAPULET and NURSE]*
CAPULET	Dew falls after sunset, but the death of Tybalt, my brother's son, brings down a torrent of rain. What's this? Still crying, girl? Still pouring tears? Your small body seems like a boat on a windy sea. Your eyes, like an ocean, rise and fall with tears. Your body, like a boat, sails on the flood. Your sighs along with your crying will sink you. Well, wife, have you delivered my orders to Juliet?
LADY	Yes, but she rejects them. I wish the foolish girl were wedded to her grave!

ACT III

TRANSLATION

CAPULET	Soft! take me with you, take me with you, wife.
	How? Will she none? Doth she not give us thanks?
	Is she not proud? Doth she not count her blest,
	Unworthy as she is, that we have wrought 145
	So worthy a gentleman to be her bride?
JULIET	Not proud you have, but thankful that you have.
	Proud can I never be of what I hate,
	But thankful even for hate that is meant love.
CAPULET	How, how, how, how, chopped-logic? What is this? 150
	'Proud'—and 'I thank you'—and 'I thank you not'—
	And yet 'not proud'? Mistress minion you,
	Thank me no thankings, nor proud me no prouds,
	But fettle your fine joints 'gainst Thursday next
	To go with Paris to Saint Peter's Church, 155
	Or I will drag thee on a hurdle thither.
	Out, you green-sickness carrion! out, you baggage!
	You tallow-face!
LADY	Fie, fie! what, are you mad?
JULIET	Good father, I beseech you on my knees,
	Hear me with patience but to speak a word. 160
CAPULET	Hang thee, young baggage! disobedient wretch!
	I tell thee what—get thee to church a Thursday
	Or never after look me in the face.
	Speak not, reply not, do not answer me!
	My fingers itch. Wife, we scarce thought us blest 165
	That God had lent us but this only child;
	But now I see this one is one too much,
	And that we have a curse in having her.
	Out on her, hilding!
NURSE	God in heaven bless her!
	You are to blame, my lord, to rate her so. 170
CAPULET	And why, my Lady Wisdom? Hold your tongue,
	Good Prudence. Smatter with your gossips, go!
NURSE	I speak no treason.
CAPULET	O, God-i-god-en!
NURSE	May not one speak?
CAPULET	Peace, you mumbling fool!
	Utter your gravity o'er a gossip's bowl, 175
	For here we need it not.

ORIGINAL

CAPULET	Explain your words, wife. Is Juliet rejecting the marriage proposal. Is she not thankful? Is she not proud of such a match? Doesn't she feel blessed that so unworthy a girl should be the bride of so noble a gentleman?
JULIET	I am grateful, but not proud of your choice. I could never be proud of so loathsome a man.
CAPULET	What is this babble? "Proud" and "thankful" and "no thank you"— and "not proud"? Little miss Juliet, spare me your thanks and your pride. Prepare youself for a wedding to Paris next Thursday at Saint Peter's Church or I will drag you there on a plank. Out with you, whimperer! Out, you hussy! Miss white-face!
LADY	Shame, shame, husband, are you crazy?
JULIET	Good father, I beg you on my knees that you listen to me.
CAPULET	Hang you, young hussy! disobedient wretch! I tell you again—go to the church on Thursday or I will never see you again. Hush. Not another word! My fingers itch to slap you. Wife, we felt unblessed that God gave us only one child. But I think one was too many. She cursed us. Out with you, worthless girl!
NURSE	God bless her! You are wrong, my lord, to berate her so.
CAPULET	How dare you interrupt, Lady Wisdom. Be silent if you are wise. Go chat with your gossipy friends!
NURSE	I have a right to disagree.
CAPULET	God give you a good evening!
NURSE	Can't I speak the truth?
CAPULET	Quiet, you mumbling fool! Speak your advice to the gossip. We don't need your meddling.

ACT III

TRANSLATION

LADY	You are too hot.
CAPULET	God's bread! it makes me mad.
	Day, night; hour, tide, time; work, play;
	Alone, in company; still my care hath been
	To have her matched; and having now provided 180
	A gentleman of noble parentage,
	Of fair demesnes, youthful, and nobly trained,
	Stuffed, as they say, with honorable parts,
	Proportioned as one's thought would wish a man—
	And then to have a wretched puling fool, 185
	A whining mammet, in her fortune's tender,
	To answer 'I'll not wed, I cannot love;
	I am too young, I pray you pardon me'!
	But, an you will not wed, I'll pardon you!
	Graze where you will, you shall not house with me. 190
	Look to't, think on't; I do not use to jest.
	Thursday is near; lay hand on heart, advise:
	An you be mine, I'll give you to my friend;
	An you be not, hang, beg, starve, die in the streets,
	For, by my soul, I'll ne'er acknowledge thee, 195
	Nor what is mine shall never do thee good.
	Trust to't. Bethink you. I'll not be forsworn.
	[Exit]
JULIET	Is there no pity in the clouds
	That sees into the bottom of my grief?
	O sweet my mother, cast me not away! 200
	Delay this marriage for a month, a week;
	Or if you do not, make the bridal bed
	In that dim monument where Tybalt lies.
LADY	Talk not to me, for I'll not speak a word.
	Do as thou wilt, for I have done with thee. 205
	[Exit]
JULIET	O God!—O nurse, how shall this be prevented?
	My husband is on earth, my faith in heaven.
	How shall that faith return again to earth
	Unless that husband send it me from heaven
	By leaving earth? Comfort me, counsel me. 210
	Alack, alack, that heaven should practise stratagems
	Upon so soft a subject as myself!
	What say'st thou? Hast thou not a word of joy?
	Some comfort, nurse.

ORIGINAL

LADY *[To her husband]* You are over-angry.

CAPULET God's communion bread! I am furious. I tried to find her a worthy mate. I found a nobleman of good family. Paris is handsome, young, well educated, honorable as a man can be. And then to have a wretched weeping fool, a whining ninny, reject good luck. How dare she reply, "I'll not marry him. I can't love him." If I were an inexperienced father, I would ask you pardon. But if you refuse this proposal, I will tell you about asking for pardon. Live where you want. You will leave this house. Think about your options. I am not joking. Thursday is coming. Search your heart. If you are my daughter, I will wed you to Paris. If you aren't my daughter, then be hanged or starve in the streets. On my soul, I will ignore you and leave you none of my property. Trust me. Think over your response. I won't break my contract with Paris. *[CAPULET goes out]*

ACT III

JULIET Does heaven have no pity on me in the depths of my sorrow? Sweet mother, don't force me away! Postpone the wedding for a month, a week. If you don't, you may bury me with Tybalt.

LADY Don't beg me. I won't speak on your behalf to your father. Do what you want. I give up on you. *[The mother goes out]*

JULIET Oh God—Oh nurse, how can I stop this wedding? I trust God that my husband is still alive. How can I trust God unless the husband he sent me dies? Comfort me, advise me. How can heaven trick so innocent a person as me! What do you say? Do you have some good news, some comfort for me?

TRANSLATION

NURSE	Faith, here it is.
	Romeo is banished; and all the world to nothing 215
	That he dares ne'er come back to challenge you;
	Or if he do, it needs must be by stealth.
	Then, since the case so stands as now it doth,
	I think it best you married with the County.
	O, he's a lovely gentleman! 220
	Romeo's a dishclout to him. An eagle, madam,
	Hath not so green, so quick, so fair an eye
	As Paris hath. Beshrew my very heart,
	I think you are happy in this second match,
	For it excels your first; or if it did not, 225
	Your first is dead—or 'twere as good he were
	As living here and you no use of him.
JULIET	Speak'st thou from thy heart?
NURSE	And from my soul too; else beshrew them both.
JULIET	Amen! 230
NURSE	What?
JULIET	Well, thou hast comforted me marvellous much.
	Go in; and tell my lady I am gone,
	Having displeased my father, to Laurence' cell,
	To make confession and to be absolved. 235
NURSE	Marry, I will; and this is wisely done.
	[Exit]
JULIET	Ancient damnation! O most wicked fiend!
	Is it more sin to wish me thus forsworn,
	Or to dispraise my lord with that same tongue
	Which she hath praised him with above compare 240
	So many thousand times? Go, counsellor!
	Thou and my bosom henceforth shall be twain.
	I'll to the friar to know his remedy.
	If all else fail, myself have power to die.
	[Exit]

ORIGINAL

NURSE	Here is my opinion. Romeo is in exile. There is no chance that he will come back to demand his rights to you. If he does come back, he must sneak into Verona. In this predicament, you would be wise to marry Paris. He's a lovely man! Romeo's a dishcloth by comparison to him. An eagle is not so green-eyed and handsome as Paris. I truly believe that this second match will please you. Paris is a better choice than Romeo, who is as good as dead in exile.
JULIET	Do you speak from the heart?
NURSE	And from the soul. Or else, confound both heart and soul.
JULIET	So be it!
NURSE	So be what?
JULIET	You have given marvelous counsel. Tell my mother that I am going to Friar Laurence's room. I must confess and be forgiven for vexing my father.
NURSE	I will. You have made a wise decision. *[The nurse goes out]*
JULIET	Satan, you wicked fiend! Is it more sinful to break my marriage vows or to malign Romeo, whom the nurse once did praise? Go, confidante! You and I are parted forever. I will go to Friar Laurence to ask you solution to this problem. If I can't solve it, I will kill myself. *[Juliet goes out]*

ACT III

TRANSLATION

ACT IV, SCENE 1

Verona. Friar Laurence's cell.

[Enter FRIAR LAURENCE and COUNTY PARIS]

FRIAR	On Thursday, sir? The time is very short.
PARIS	My father Capulet will have it so, And I am nothing slow to slack his haste.
FRIAR	You say you do not know the lady's mind. Uneven is the course; I like it not.

5

PARIS	Immoderately she weeps for Tybalt's death, And therefore have I little talked of love; For Venus smiles not in a house of tears. Now, sir, her father counts it dangerous That she do give her sorrow so much sway, And in his wisdom hastes our marriage To stop the inundation of her tears, Which, too much minded by herself alone, May be put from her by society. Now do you know the reason of this haste.

10

15

FRIAR	*[Aside]* I would I knew not why it should be slowed.— Look, sir, here comes the lady toward my cell. *[Enter JULIET]*
PARIS	Happily met, my lady and my wife!
JULIET	That may be, sir, when I may be a wife.
PARIS	That 'may be' must be, love, on Thursday next.

20

JULIET	What must be shall be.
FRIAR	That's a certain text.
PARIS	Come you to make confession to this father?
JULIET	To answer that, I should confess to you.
PARIS	Do not deny to him that you love me.
JULIET	I will confess to you that I love him.

25

PARIS	So will ye, I am sure, that you love me.
JULIET	If I do so, it will be of more price, Being spoke behind your back, than to your face.
PARIS	Poor soul, thy face is much abused with tears.

ORIGINAL

ACT IV, SCENE 1

In Verona at Friar Laurence's room.

[FRIAR LAURENCE enters with COUNT PARIS]

FRIAR	You want to marry on Thursday, sir? That doesn't leave much time.
PARIS	My future father-in-law Capulet chose the date. I have no wish to wait longer for the wedding.
FRIAR	You haven't asked Juliet if she is willing. I don't like to proceed without the bride's opinion.
PARIS	She mourns Tybalt to excess. I have not brought up the subject of marriage. The goddess of passion does not bless a mournful household. Her father thinks it is harmful for Juliet to sink into heavy mourning. He believes that our marriage will end her sorrow. She stays too long in solitude. He thinks my company will gladden her. That is why I am in a hurry for the wedding.
FRIAR	*[To himself]* I wish that I didn't know why the wedding should be postponed. Look Paris, here comes Juliet to my room. *[Enter JULIET]*
PARIS	This is a happy encounter, my lady and my wife!
JULIET	You may be right after I am married to you.
PARIS	The wedding will be next Thursday.
JULIET	What must be will be.
FRIAR	That's a bit of wisdom.
PARIS	Did you come to Friar Laurence for confession?
JULIET	If I answer you, I would be confessing to you.
PARIS	When you confess, don't deny that you love me.
JULIET	I confess to you that I love Friar Laurence.
PARIS	I am certain that you will say that you love me.
JULIET	If I do, I will have to atone more for speaking behind your back than to your face.
PARIS	Poor soul, your face is ruined from weeping.

ACT IV

TRANSLATION

JULIET	The tears have got small victory by that,	30
	For it was bad enough before their spite.	
PARIS	Thou wrong'st it more than tears with that report.	
JULIET	That is no slander, sir, which is a truth;	
	And what I spake, I spake it to my face.	
PARIS	Thy face is mine, and thou hast sland'red it.	35
JULIET	It may be so, for it is not mine own.	
	Are you at leisure, holy father, now,	
	Or shall I come to you at evening mass?	
FRIAR	My leisure serves me, pensive daughter, now.	
	My lord, we must entreat the time alone.	40
PARIS	God shield I should disturb devotion!	
	Juliet, on Thursday early will I rouse ye.	
	Till then, adieu, and keep this holy kiss. *[Exit]*	
JULIET	O, shut the door! and when thou hast done so,	
	Come weep with me—past hope, past cure, past help!	45
FRIAR	Ah, Juliet, I already know thy grief;	
	It strains me past the compass of my wits.	
	I hear thou must, and nothing may prorogue it,	
	On Thursday next be married to this County.	
JULIET	Tell me not, friar, that thou hearest of this,	50
	Unless thou tell me how I may prevent it.	
	If in thy wisdom thou canst give no help,	
	Do thou but call my resolution wise	
	And with this knife I'll help it presently.	
	God joined my heart and Romeo's, thou our hands;	55
	And ere this hand, by thee to Romeo's sealed,	
	Shall be the label to another deed,	
	Or my true heart with treacherous revolt	
	Turn to another, this shall slay them both.	
	Therefore, out of thy long-experienced time,	60
	Give me some present counsel; or, behold,	
	'Twixt my extremes and me this bloody knife	
	Shall play the umpire, arbitrating that	
	Which the commission of thy years and art	
	Could to no issue of true honor bring.	65
	Be not so long to speak. I long to die	
	If what thou speak'st speak not of remedy.	

ORIGINAL

JULIET	Tears have won a small victory by ruining my face. It was ugly enough before the tears.
PARIS	You are wrong to say so.
JULIET	It is true, sir. What I said, I said to my own face.
PARIS	The face you slandered belongs to me.
JULIET	Maybe so, for my face doesn't belong to me. Are you free now, holy father, or shall I return at evening Mass?
FRIAR	I am free now, sad girl. My lord, she and I must have privacy.
PARIS	God prevent me from interrupting her confession! Juliet, on Thursday morning, I will awaken you. Until then, farewell, and keep this holy kiss. *[Paris goes out]*
JULIET	Oh, shut the door. When it is closed, weep with me—I am past hope, past remedy, past help!
FRIAR	Ah, Juliet, I already know the cause of your grief. I have strained my mind thinking up a solution. I hear that you must marry. Nothing can postpone it. On Thursday, you must wed Count Paris.
JULIET	Don't tell me, Friar Laurence, that you know of the plans unless you can tell me how to stop the marriage. If you can't help me, I will stab myself with this knife. God joined my heart to Romeo's heart. You joined our hands. Before the hand that you gave to Romeo accepts another marriage. Or my honest heart betrays Romeo, I will kill both my heart and myself. From your long experience, give me some advice. Or in front of your eyes, this knife will release me from my dilemma. Death will decide the quandary that your wisdom could not honorably settle. Don't take too long. I long to die if you can't propose a solution.

ACT IV

FRIAR   Hold, daughter. I do spy a kind of hope,
               Which craves as desperate an execution
               As that is desperate which we would prevent.   70
               If, rather than to marry County Paris,
               Thou hast the strength of will to slay thyself,
               Then is it likely thou wilt undertake
               A thing like death to chide away this shame,
               That cop'st with death himself to scape from it;   75
               And, if thou darest, I'll give thee remedy.

JULIET   O, bid me leap, rather than marry Paris,
               From off the battlements of any tower,
               Or walk in thievish ways, or bid me lurk
               Where serpents are; chain me with roaring bears,   80
               Or hide me nightly in a charnel house,
               O'ercovered quite with dead men's rattling bones,
               With reeky shanks and yellow chapless skulls;
               Or bid me go into a new-made grave
               And hide me with a dead man in his shroud—   85
               Things that, to hear them told, have made me tremble—
               And I will do it without fear or doubt,
               To live an unstained wife to my sweet love.

FRIAR   Hold, then. Go home, be merry, give consent
               To marry Paris. Wednesday is tomorrow.   90
               Tomorrow night look that thou lie alone;
               Let not the nurse lie with thee in thy chamber.
               Take thou this vial, being then in bed,
               And this distilling liquor drink thou off;
               When presently through all thy veins shall run   95
               A cold and drowsy humor; for no pulse
               Shall keep his native progress, but surcease;
               No warmth, no breath, shall testify thou livest;
               The roses in thy lips and cheeks shall fade
               To wanny ashes, thy eyes' windows fall   100
               Like death when he shuts up the day of life;
               Each part, deprived of supple government,
               Shall, stiff and stark and cold, appear like death;
               And in this borrowed likeness of shrunk death
               Thou shalt continue two-and-forty hours,   105
               And then awake as from a pleasant sleep.
               Now, when the bridegroom in the morning comes
               To rouse thee from thy bed, there art thou dead.
               Then, as the manner of our country is,
               In thy best robes uncovered on the bier   110
               Thou shalt be borne to that same ancient vault
               Where all the kindred of the Capulets lie.

ORIGINAL

FRIAR   Wait, Juliet. I see a ray of hope. My proposal is as daring as your choice of suicide. I hope to save your life. If you are desperate enough to kill yourself rather than marry Count Paris, then you might be willing to follow a plan to make you appear dead. You can forestall death by accepting my daring solution.

JULIET   Tell me to jump off a tower rather than marry Paris. Or have me walk among criminals or among snakes. Chain me up with bears. Or conceal me in a mortuary among skeletons with smelly bones and lipless skulls. Tell me to hide in a grave within the burial cloth of a dead man. Tell me anything that will make me tremble—I will obey you without fear or hesitation if I may live a faithful wife to Romeo.

FRIAR   Don't do anything drastic. Act happy. Agree to marry Paris. On Wednesday night, sleep alone. Make your nurse leave you alone in your room. Go to bed and drink the fluid from this bottle. It will immediately course through your veins with a cold, sleep-inducing effect. Your pulse will slacken. No warmth, no breathing will prove that you are alive. Your rosy lips and cheeks will grow pale, your eyes will look dead. Every part of your body, deprived of life, will stiffen and chill like a corpse. This death-like state will last forty-two hours. Then you will wake up as though from sleep. When Paris comes on Thursday morning to awaken you, you will seem dead. As is the custom in Verona, your family will dress you in your best and carry you uncovered to the Capulet family vault.

ACT IV

In the mean time, against thou shalt awake,
Shall Romeo by my letters know our drift;
And hither shall he come; and he and I   115
Will watch thy waking, and that very night
Shall Romeo bear thee hence to Mantua.
And this shall free thee from this present shame,
If no inconstant toy nor womanish fear
Abate thy valor in the acting it.   120

JULIET   Give me, give me! O, tell not me of fear!

FRIAR   Hold! Get you gone, be strong and prosperous
In this resolve. I'll send a friar with speed
To Mantua, with my letters to thy lord.

JULIET   Love give me strength! and strength shall help afford.   125
Farewell, dear father. *[Exit with Friar]*

ORIGINAL

Meanwhile, before you awaken, I will inform Romeo of your state in a letter. He will come and he and I will wait for you to awaken. That night, he will take you away to Mantua. This plan will free you from a second marriage. If you do as I ask, agree to this bold plan.

JULIET   Give me the drug. Don't worry that I am too afraid to drink it!

FRIAR   Go home. Be strong in a plan that will benefit you. I will send a friar quickly to Mantua with a letter for Romeo.

JULIET   Love, make me strong! Strength will aid me. Farewell, dear father. *[JULIET departs with FRIAR LAURENCE]*

TRANSLATION

ACT IV, SCENE 2

The same. Hall in Capulet's house.

[Enter CAPULET, MOTHER, NURSE, and Servingmen, two or three]

CAPULET	So many guests invite as here are writ.
	[Exit a Servingman]
	Sirrah, go hire me twenty cunning cooks.
SERVINGMAN	You shall have none ill, Sir; for I'll
	try if they can lick their fingers.
CAPULET	How canst thou try them so?
SERVINGMAN	Marry, sir, 'tis an ill cook that cannot
	lick his own fingers. Therefore he that cannot lick
	his fingers goes not with me.
CAPULET	Go, begone. *[Exit Servingman]*
	We shall be much unfurnished for this time.
	What, is my daughter gone to Friar Laurence?
NURSE	Ay, forsooth.
CAPULET	Well, he may chance to do some good on her.
	A peevish self-willed harlotry it is.
	[Enter JULIET]
NURSE	See where she comes from shrift with merry look.
CAPULET	How now, my headstrong? Where have you been
	gadding?
JULIET	Where I have learnt me to repent the sin
	Of disobedient opposition
	To you and your behests, and am enjoined
	By holy Laurence to fall prostrate here
	To beg your pardon. Pardon, I beseech you!
	Henceforward I am ever ruled by you.
CAPULET	Send for the County. Go tell him of this.
	I'll have this knot knit up tomorrow morning.
JULIET	I met the youthful lord at Laurence' cell
	And gave him what becomed love I might,
	Not stepping o'er the bounds of modesty.

Line numbers: 5, 10, 15, 20, 25

ORIGINAL

ACT IV, SCENE 2

That same day in the hall of the Capulet house.

[Enter CAPULET, MOTHER, NURSE, and Servingmen, two or three]

CAPULET	The guest list is written here. *[The servant departs to invite them]* Sir, go hire twenty clever cooks for the wedding.
SERVINGMAN	You will have no bad ones, sir. I will test them by having them lick their food from their fingers.
CAPULET	What will that prove?
SERVINGMAN	It is a poor cook who won't lick his own cooking from his fingers. If he can't lick his fingers, I won't select him.
CAPULET	Go on your way. *[The servant departs]* We don't have enough time to get ready. Has Juliet gone to Friar Laurence?
NURSE	Yes.
CAPULET	Perhaps he will improve her mood. She is irritable and willful. *[JULIET enters]*
NURSE	She returns from confession with a smiling face.
CAPULET	How are you, my headstrong girl? Where have you been?
JULIET	I have decided to repent of disobeying your orders. Friar Laurence urges me to humble myself and ask your forgiveness. Please pardon me. From here on, I will do as you say.
CAPULET	Send for Count Paris. Tell him of Juliet's change of heart. I will have you two marry tomorrow morning.
JULIET	I encountered Paris at Friar Laurence's room and promised him to be loving. I still maintained my modesty.

ACT IV

TRANSLATION

CAPULET	Why, I am glad on't. This is well. Stand up.
	This is as't should be. Let me see the County. 30
	Ay, marry, go, I say, and fetch him hither.
	Now, afore God, this reverend holy friar,
	All our whole city is much bound to him.
JULIET	Nurse, will you go with me into my closet
	To help me sort such needful ornaments 35
	As you think fit to furnish me tomorrow?
MOTHER	No, not till Thursday. There is time enough.
CAPULET	Go, nurse, go with her. We'll to church tomorrow.
	[Exeunt JULIET and NURSE]
MOTHER	We shall be short in our provision.
	'Tis now near night.
CAPULET	Tush, I will stir about, 40
	And all things shall be well, I warrant thee, wife.
	Go thou to Juliet, help to deck up her.
	I'll not to bed tonight; let me alone.
	I'll play the housewife for this once. What, ho!
	They are all forth; well, I will walk myself 45
	To County Paris, to prepare up him
	Against tomorrow. My heart is wondrous light,
	Since this same wayward girl is so reclaimed.
	[Exit with MOTHER]

CAPULET   I am glad to hear it. This is good. Stand up. This behavior is as it should be. I want to see Count Paris. Go. Bring him here. Before God, the city of Verona owes much to this reverend holy friar.

JULIET   Nurse, will you accompany me to my closet and help me choose a suitable ensemble for my wedding tomorrow?

MOTHER   No, the wedding is Thursday. There is plenty of time to choose an outfit.

CAPULET   Go with her, nurse. We will go to church tomorrow. *[JULIET and the NURSE depart]*

MOTHER   We will be short of food. It is nearly night.

CAPULET   Hush. I will get moving. Everything will work out, I guarantee, wife. You go with Juliet and help her dress. I will stay up all night. Leave me alone. I will be the housewife for this occasion. Where is a servant? They are all out on errands. I will go myself to Count Paris to ready him for tomorrow. My heart feels light since Juliet has stopped disobeying me. *[He departs with his wife]*

ACT IV

TRANSLATION

ACT IV, SCENE 3

The same. Juliet's chamber.

[Enter JULIET and NURSE]

JULIET
Ay, those attires are best; but, gentle nurse,
I pray thee leave me to myself to-night;
For I have need of many orisons
To move the heavens to smile upon my state,
Which, well thou knowest, is cross and full of sin.   5
[Enter MOTHER]

MOTHER
What, are you busy, ho? Need you my help?

JULIET
No, madam; we have culled such necessaries
As are behoveful for our state to-morrow.
So please you, let me now be left alone,
And let the nurse this night sit up with you;   10
For I am sure you have your hands full all
In this so sudden business.

MOTHER
                            Good night.
Get thee to bed, and rest; for thou hast need.
[Exeunt MOTHER and NURSE]

JULIET
Farewell! God knows when we shall meet again.
I have a faint cold fear thrills through my veins   15
That almost freezes up the heat of life.
I'll call them back again to comfort me.
Nurse!—What should she do here?
My dismal scene I needs must act alone.
Come, vial.   20
What if this mixture do not work at all?
Shall I be married then to-morrow morning?
No, no! This shall forbid it. Lie thou there.
[Lays down a dagger]
What if it be a poison which the friar
Subtly hath minist'red to have me dead,   25
Lest in this marriage he should be dishonored
Because he married me before to Romeo?
I fear it is; and yet methinks it should not,
For he hath still been tried a holy man.
How if, when I am laid into the tomb,   30
I wake before the time that Romeo
Come to redeem me? There's a fearful point!

ORIGINAL

ACT IV, SCENE 3

That same night in Juliet's room.

[Enter JULIET and NURSE]

JULIET   Yes, this choice makes a good wedding outfit. Sweet nurse, please leave me alone tonight. I have many prayers to ask God to bless my marriage. You know that I tend to be cross and sinful. *[Her mother enters]*

MOTHER   Are you busy? Do you need my help?

JULIET   No, ma'am. We have chosen what I should wear tomorrow as a bride-to-be. Leave me to myself and have the nurse sit up with you tonight. I am certain that you are busy with this abrupt wedding to plan for.

MOTHER   Good night. Go to bed and rest. You need some sleep. *[The mother and nurse go out]*

JULIET   Goodbye. God knows when we will meet again. I feel a chill fear in my veins that almost freezes my blood. I will call them back to comfort me. Nurse! What could she do for me? This terrifying death scene I must act alone. Here is the bottle. What if this drug doesn't work? Will I have to marry Paris tomorrow morning? No. This plan will forbid marriage to Paris. Dagger, lie near by. *[Lays down a dagger]* What if Friar Laurence has given me poison to kill me! Would he kill me to save himself from dishonor for performing my marriage to Romeo? I fear it is poison. But he wouldn't kill me, for the friar is a holy man. What if I wake in the Capulet vault before Romeo comes for me? What a terrifying thought!

ACT IV

Shall I not then be stifled in the vault,
To whose foul mouth no healthsome air breathes in,
And there die strangled ere my Romeo comes?   35
Or, if I live, is it not very like
The horrible conceit of death and night,
Together with the terror of the place—
As in a vault, an ancient receptacle
Where for this many hundred years the bones   40
Of all my buried ancestors are packed;
Where bloody Tybalt, yet but green in earth,
Lies fest'ring in his shroud; where, as they say,
At some hours in the night spirits resort—
Alack, alack, is it not like that I,   45
So early waking—what with loathsome smells,
And shrikes like mandrakes' torn out of the earth,
That living mortals, hearing them, run mad—
O, if I wake, shall I not be distraught,
Environed with all these hideous fears,   50
And madly play with my forefathers' joints,
And pluck the mangled Tybalt from his shroud,
And, in this rage, with some great kinsman's bone
As with a club dash out my desp'rate brains?
O, look! methinks I see my cousin's ghost   55
Seeking out Romeo, that did spit his body
Upon a rapier's point. Stay, Tybalt, stay!
Romeo, I come! this do I drink to thee.
[She falls upon her bed within the curtains]

ORIGINAL

Would I be stifled in the vault in the foul air? Would I suffocate before Romeo comes? If I live, the thought of death and dark, together with the horrors of a burial vault, an old storage place for dead ancestors left inside over many centuries. . . . Where Tybalt, newly dead, lies rotting in his burial cloth. . . . Where, it is said that at some time in the night ghosts enter. . . . I may awaken early amid loathsome odors and shrieks and go crazy. If I awaken, would I be terrified around such terrors? Would I play insanely with ancestors' bones and yank Tybalt from his burial cloth? Might I go mad and dash out my brains by using a relative's bone as a club? I think I see Tybalt's ghost looking for Romeo, who speared his body on a sword point. Stay, Tybalt, stay! Romeo, I'm coming to you. I drink this drug for you. *[JULIET falls between the bed curtains and onto the mattress]*

ACT IV

TRANSLATION

ACT IV, SCENE 4

The same. Hall in Capulet's house.

[Enter LADY of the House and NURSE]

LADY   Hold, take these keys and fetch more spices, nurse.

NURSE   They call for dates and quinces in the pastry.
                 [Enter old CAPULET]

CAPULET   Come, stir, stir, stir! The second cock hath crowed,
                 The curfew bell hath rung, 'tis three o'clock.
                 Look to the baked meats, good Angelica;   5
                 Spare not for cost.

NURSE   Go, you cot-quean, go,
                 Get you to bed! Faith, you'll be sick tomorrow
                 For this night's watching.

CAPULET   No, not a whit. What, I have watched ere now
                 All night for lesser cause, and ne'er been sick.   10

LADY   Ay, you have been a mouse-hunt in your time;
                 But I will watch you from such watching now.
                 [Exit LADY and NURSE]

CAPULET   A jealous hood, a jealous hood!
                 [Enter three or four Fellows with spits and logs and baskets]
                 Now, fellow,
                 What is there?

FIRST FELLOW Things for the cook, sir; but I know not what.   15

CAPULET   Make haste, make haste. *[Exit first Fellow]*
                   Sirrah, fetch drier logs.
                 Call Peter; he will show thee where they are.

SECOND FELLOW I have a head, sir, that will find out logs
                 And never trouble Peter for the matter.

ACT IV, SCENE 4

The same night in a hall of the Capulet house.

[Enter LADY of the House and NURSE]

LADY   Take these keys and bring more spices, nurse.

NURSE   You need dates and quinces in the pastry. *[Enter old CAPULET]*

CAPULET   Come, get a move on! It is near dawn. The curfew bell rang at 3:00 A.M. Angelica, check on the meat in the oven. Spare no cost.

NURSE   Go, you meddler, go. Get to bed! You will make yourself sick tomorrow if you stay up all night.

CAPULET   No, not a chance. I have stayed up all night for less important causes and I wasn't sick.

LADY   You have chased women in your day. I will keep watch over you now. *[LADY CAPULET and the NURSE go out]*

CAPULET   Jealousy, jealousy! *[Three or four men enter with barbecue spits, logs, and baskets]* What is this for?

FIRST FELLOW   Things the cook needs, sir. I don't know what for.

CAPULET   Hurry, hurry. *[The first man goes out]* Sir, bring drier wood for the oven. Call Peter. He will show you where to find it.

SECOND FELLOW I am smart enough to find dry logs without asking Peter for help.

TRANSLATION

CAPULET   Mass, and well said; a merry whoreson, ha!   20
                            Thou shalt be loggerhead.
                            [Exit second Fellow, with the others]
                                           Good Father! 'tis day.
                            The County will be here with music straight,
                            For so he said he would. [Play music] I hear him near.
                            Nurse! Wife! What, ho! What, nurse, I say!
                            [Enter NURSE]
                            Go waken Juliet; go and trim her up.   25
                            I'll go and chat with Paris. Hie, make haste,
                            Make haste! The bridegroom he is come already:
                            Make haste, I say. *[Exit]*

CAPULET   Well put, you jolly bastard! You will be a blockhead.
[The second man goes out with the other servants]
Heavenly Father! It's already day. Count Paris will be here
with musicians soon, as he promised. *[Play music]* He is
coming. Nurse! Wife! Where is everybody? Nurse, I say!
[Enter NURSE] Get Juliet out of bed and dress her. I'll go
and chat with Paris. Hurry! The groom is already here.
Hurry! *[CAPULET goes out]*

TRANSLATION

ACT IV, SCENE 5

The same. Juliet's chamber.

[NURSE goes to curtains]

NURSE	Mistress! what, mistress! Juliet! Fast, I warrant her, she.
	Why, lamb! why, lady! Fie, you slug-abed.
	Why, love, I say! madam! sweetheart! Why, bride!
	What, not a word? You take your pennyworths now;
	Sleep for a week; for the next night, I warrant, 5
	The County Paris hath set up his rest
	That you shall rest but little. God forgive me!
	Marry, and amen. How sound is she asleep!
	I needs must wake her. Madam, madam, madam!
	Ay, let the County take you in your bed; 10
	He'll fright you up, i' faith. Will it not be?
	[Draws aside the curtains]
	What, dressed, and in your clothes, and down again?
	I must needs wake you. Lady! lady! lady!
	Alas, alas! Help, help! my lady's dead!
	O weraday that ever I was born! 15
	Some aqua vitae, ho! My lord! my lady!
	[Enter MOTHER]

MOTHER	What noise is here?
NURSE	O lamentable day!
MOTHER	What is the matter?
NURSE	Look, look! O heavy day!
MOTHER	O me, O me! My child, my only life!
	Revive, look up, or I will die with thee! 20
	Help, help! Call help.
	[Enter CAPULET]
CAPULET	For shame, bring Juliet forth; her lord is come.
NURSE	She's dead, deceased; she's dead, alack the day!
MOTHER	Alack the day, she's dead, she's dead, she's dead!
CAPULET	Ha! let me see her. Out alas! she's cold, 25
	Her blood is settled, and her joints are stiff;
	Life and these lips have long been separated.
	Death lies on her like an untimely frost
	Upon the sweetest flower of all the field.

ORIGINAL

ACT IV, SCENE 5

The same morning in Juliet's room.

[NURSE goes to curtains]

NURSE   Mistress! Juliet! Fast asleep, I guarantee. Why lamb!
Lady! Shame, you slug-a-bed. Love, madam, sweetheart!
Why, bride! Not a word from you? Sleep while you can.
Tonight, I promise, Count Paris will give you little rest.
God forgive my vulgarity. She is so soundly asleep! I must
shake her. Madam! If the Count finds you still in bed,
he'll scare you up. Isn't that so? *[Draws aside the curtains]*
Dressed and fallen asleep again? I must awaken you.
Lady! Alas! Help, my lady's dead! Oh alas that I was born!
Some brandy. My lord, my lady! *[Enter MOTHER]*

MOTHER   Why all this noise?

NURSE   Oh sorrowful day!

MOTHER   What is the matter?

NURSE   Look, look! Oh grievous day!

MOTHER   Oh me! My child, my only child! Wake up, look at me, or
I will die with you! Help, get help! *[Enter CAPULET]*

CAPULET   For shame, call Juliet. Her groom is here.

NURSE   She's dead!

MOTHER   Oh woeful day, she's dead!

CAPULET   Let me look at her. Gone! She is cold, her blood settled,
and her joints stiff. Life is long gone from these lips.
Death lies on her like an early frost on the tenderest
flower in the field.

TRANSLATION

NURSE	O lamentable day!
MOTHER	O woeful time! 30
CAPULET	Death, that hath ta'en her hence to make me wail,
	Ties up my tongue and will not let me speak.
	[Enter FRIAR LAURENCE and the COUNTY PARIS,
	with Musicians]
FRIAR	Come, is the bride ready to go to church?
CAPULET	Ready to go, but never to return.
	O son, the night before thy wedding day 35
	Hath Death lain with thy wife. There she lies,
	Flower as she was, deflowered by him.
	Death is my son-in-law, Death is my heir;
	My daughter he hath wedded. I will die
	And leave him all. Life, living, all is Death's. 40
PARIS	Have I thought long to see this morning's face,
	And doth it give me such a sight as this?
MOTHER	Accursed, unhappy, wretched, hateful day!
	Most miserable hour that e'er time saw
	In lasting labor of his pilgrimage! 45
	But one, poor one, one poor and loving child,
	But one thing to rejoice and solace in,
	And cruel Death hath catched it from my sight.
NURSE	O woe! O woeful, woeful, woeful day!
	Most lamentable day, most woeful day 50
	That ever ever I did yet behold!
	O day, O day, O day! O hateful day!
	Never was seen so black a day as this.
	O woeful day! O woeful day!
PARIS	Beguiled, divorced, wronged, spited, slain! 55
	Most detestable Death, by thee beguiled,
	By cruel, cruel thee quite overthrown.
	O love! O life! not life, but love in death!
CAPULET	Despised, distressed, hated, martyred, killed!
	Uncomfortable time, why cam'st thou now 60
	To murder, murder our solemnity?
	O child, O child! my soul, and not my child!
	Dead art thou—alack, my child is dead,
	And with my child my joys are buried!

ORIGINAL

NURSE	Oh lamentable day!
MOTHER	Oh grievous time!
CAPULET	Her death makes me want to wail, but my tongue is silent. *[Enter FRIAR LAURENCE and the COUNTY PARIS, with Musicians]*
FRIAR	Is the bride ready for the ceremony?
CAPULET	She is ready to go to church, but never to return. Oh Paris, the night before your wedding, death took your bride. There she lies, a flower plucked by death. Death is her groom. Death is my heir. My daughter is gone. I will die and leave all to death. All life belongs to death.
PARIS	I have long anticipated her face this morning. I didn't expect this sight.
MOTHER	Damned, miserable, hateful day! Most wretched hour that day has ever brought! I have only one child to comfort and delight me and death has taken her away.
NURSE	Oh grief! Oh grievous day! Most sorrowful day, most grievous day that I have ever seen! Oh miserable day! There was never a day as dark as this one. Oh grievous day!
PARIS	Tricked, separated, wronged, despised, killed! Tricked by death, by cruel fate ended. Oh love! Oh life, gone forever!
CAPULET	Hated, troubled, loathed, sacrificed, killed! Comfortless time, why did you come now to destroy our ceremony? Oh child! my soul, who is no longer my daughter! You are gone—my child is gone. With her passing my joy is buried!

TRANSLATION

FRIAR	Peace, ho, for shame! Confusion's cure lives not 65
	In these confusions. Heaven and yourself
	Had part in this fair maid—now heaven hath all,
	And all the better is it for the maid.
	Your part in her you could not keep from death,
	But heaven keeps his part in eternal life. 70
	The most you sought was her promotion,
	For 'twas your heaven she should be advanced;
	And weep ye now, seeing she is advanced
	Above the clouds, as high as heaven itself?
	O, in this love, you love your child so ill 75
	That you run mad, seeing that she is well.
	She's not well married that lives married long,
	But she's best married that dies married young.
	Dry up your tears and stick your rosemary
	On this fair corse, and, as the custom is, 80
	In all her best array bear her to church;
	For though fond nature bids us all lament,
	Yet nature's tears are reason's merriment.

CAPULET All things that we ordained festival
Turn from their office to black funeral—   85
Our instruments to melancholy bells,
Our wedding cheer to a sad burial feast;
Our solemn hymns to sullen dirges change;
Our bridal flowers serve for buried corse;
And all things change them to the contrary.   90

FRIAR Sir, go you in; and, madam, go with him;
And go, Sir Paris. Every one prepare
To follow this fair corse unto her grave.
The heavens do low'r upon you for some ill;
Move them no more by crossing their high will.   95
*[Exeunt casting rosemary on her and shutting the
curtains. Manet the Nurse with Musicians]*

FIRST MUSICIAN Faith, we may put up our pipes and be gone.

NURSE Honest good fellows, ah, put up, put up!
For well you know this is a pitiful case. *[Exit]*

FIRST MUSICIAN Ay, by my troth, the case may be amended.
[Enter PETER]

PETER Musicians, O, musicians, 'Heart's ease,' 'Heart's   100
ease'! O, an you will have me live, play 'Heart's ease.'

FIRST MUSICIAN Why 'Heart's ease'?

ORIGINAL

FRIAR	Quiet, for shame! Your solace lies not in chaos. You and heaven made this fair girl—now heaven takes all of her. The girl is in a better place. Her human side was bound to die, but heaven keeps her soul forever. At most, you wanted her to prosper, but heaven advanced her to the eternal. Why do you weep when you see that she has risen to heaven? You let your love turn to frenzy when you should be glad that she is in heaven. She is not happiest who lives out a long marriage. She is most fortunate for dying young. Dry your tears. Deck her body with rosemary. Dress her well and carry her to church. Although it is natural to mourn, yet logic tells us otherwise.
CAPULET	All our preparations for a wedding now suit a funeral. We must exchange music for church bells, wedding cheer for a burial feast, and solemn wedding hymns to mournful songs. The wedding flowers will serve for the burial. Everything is overturned from glad to sad.
FRIAR	Capulet, go, and, madam, accompany him. Paris, you go too. Everyone prepare for the funeral procession to the cemetery. The heavens have brought you ill fortune. Don't risk worse luck by defying God's will. *[They leave Juliet's bed, toss rosemary on her corpse, and close the bed curtains. The nurse and musicians remain behind]*
FIRST MUSICIAN	We should put up our instruments and leave.
NURSE	Musicians, put up your instruments! This is a pitiful situation. *[She departs]*
FIRST MUSICIAN	Yes. An instrument case may be mended. *[Enter PETER]*
PETER	Musicians, please play "Heart's Ease."
FIRST MUSICIAN	Why that melody?

ACT IV

TRANSLATION

PETER	O, musicians, because my heart itself plays 'My heart is full of woe.' O, play me some merry dump to comfort me. 105
FIRST MUSICIAN	Not a dump we! 'Tis no time to play now.
PETER	You will not then?
FIRST MUSICIAN	No.
PETER	I will then give it you soundly.
FIRST MUSICIAN	What will you give us? 110
PETER	No money, on my faith, but the gleek. I will give you the minstrel.
FIRST MUSICIAN	Then will I give you the serving-creature.
PETER	Then will I lay the serving-creature's dagger on your pate. I will carry no crotchets. I'll re you, I'll fa you. Do you note me? 115
FIRST MUSICIAN	An you re us and fa us, you note us.
SECOND MUSICIAN	Pray you put up your dagger, and put out your wit.
PETER	Then have at you with my wit! I will dry-beat 120 you with an iron wit, and put up my iron dagger. Answer me like men.

> *When griping grief the heart doth wound,*
> *And doleful dumps the mind oppress,*
> *Then music with her silver sound—* 125

	Why 'silver sound'? Why 'music with her silver sound'? What say you, Simon Catling?
FIRST MUSICIAN	Marry, sir, because silver hath a sweet sound.
PETER	Pretty! What say you, Hugh Rebeck?
SECOND MUSICIAN	I say 'silver sound' because musicians sound 130 for silver.
PETER	Pretty too! What say you, James Soundpost?
THIRD MUSICIAN	Faith, I know not what to say.

ORIGINAL

PETER	Oh, musicians, because I feel sorrow in my heart. Play a happy funeral song to comfort me.
FIRST MUSICIAN	We don't play funeral tunes! This is no time to play.
PETER	You won't play?
FIRST MUSICIAN	No.
PETER	I will let you have it.
FIRST MUSICIAN	What will you give us?
PETER	I will mock you and withhold your pay. I will insult you.
FIRST MUSICIAN	Then I will call you a servant.
PETER	Then I will strike your head with my dagger. I will endure no whims. I'll sing you re and fa. Do you note me?
FIRST MUSICIAN	If you re and fa us, you give us note.
SECOND MUSICIAN	Sheathe your dagger and stop your witticisms.

PETER	I will attack you with my wit! I will pummel you with my iron wit and put up my weapon. Answer me like men.
	      When painful woe wounds the heart
	      and mournful songs sadden the mind,
	      then music with her silvery sound—
	Why is sound called "silvery"? Why "music with her silvery sound"? What do you say, Simon Catgut?

FIRST MUSICIAN	Because silver makes a sweet sound.
PETER	Nice answer! What do you say, Hugh Fiddle?
SECOND MUSICIAN	I say "silvery sound" because musicians play for silver coins.
PETER	Another nice answer! What do you say, James Soundpost?
THIRD MUSICIAN	I don't know what to say.

ACT IV

TRANSLATION

PETER O, I cry you mercy, you are the singer. I will say
for you. It is 'music with her silver sound' because   135
musicians have no gold for sounding.
'Then music with her silver sound
With speedy help doth lend redress.' *[Exit]*

FIRST MUSICIAN What a pestilent knave is this same!

**SECOND
MUSICIAN** Hang him, Jack! Come, we'll in here, tarry   140
for the mourners, and stay dinner.
[Exit with others]

PETER	I beg your pardon, you are the singer. I will answer for you. Music is silvery because musicians receive no gold for playing. "Then music with her silvery sound rapidly brings comfort." *[PETER departs]*
FIRST MUSICIAN	What an obnoxious pest!
SECOND MUSICIAN	Forget him, Jack! Let's enter the hall, mingle with the mourners, and stay for dinner. *[He goes out with the others]*

TRANSLATION

ACT V, SCENE 1

Mantua. A street.

[Enter ROMEO]

ROMEO	If I may trust the flattering truth of sleep,
	My dreams presage some joyful news at hand.
	My bosom's lord sits lightly in his throne,
	And all this day an unaccustomed spirit
	Lifts me above the ground with cheerful thoughts. 5
	I dreamt my lady came and found me dead
	(Strange dream that gives a dead man leave to think!)
	And breathed such life with kisses in my lips
	That I revived and was an emperor.
	Ah me! How sweet is love itself possessed, 10
	When but love's shadows are so rich in joy!
	[Enter Romeo's Man BALTHASAR, booted]
	News from Verona! How now, Balthasar?
	Dost thou not bring me letters from the friar?
	How doth my lady? Is my father well?
	How fares my Juliet? That I ask again, 15
	For nothing can be ill if she be well.

BALTHASAR	Then she is well, and nothing can be ill.
	Her body sleeps in Capel's monument,
	And her immortal part with angels lives.
	I saw her laid low in her kindred's vault 20
	And presently took post to tell it you.
	O, pardon me for bringing these ill news,
	Since you did leave it for my office, sir.

ROMEO	Is it e'en so? Then I defy you, stars!
	Thou knowest my lodging. Get me ink and paper 25
	And hire posthorses. I will hence to-night.

BALTHASAR	I do beseech you, sir, have patience.
	Your looks are pale and wild and do import
	Some misadventure.

ROMEO	Tush, thou art deceived.
	Leave me and do the thing I bid thee do. 30
	Hast thou no letters to me from the friar?

BALTHASAR	No, my good lord.

ORIGINAL

ACT V, SCENE 1

A street in Mantua, a town some ten miles southwest of Verona, Italy.

[Enter ROMEO]

ROMEO   If I my trust my dreams, I anticipate good news. Love lives in my heart. All day, a cheerful mood has lifted me above earth with happy thoughts. I dreamed that Juliet discovered my corpse and revived me with kisses. I became an emperor. Ah me! Love is truly wonderful when even dreams of love are so joyful! *[Romeo's servant BALTHASAR enters wearing horseman's boots]* Did you bring news from Verona, Balthasar? Did you bring letters from Friar Laurence? How is my wife? Is my father well? How is Juliet? Of course, nothing can be wrong if Juliet is well.

BALTHASAR   Then she is well and nothing can be wrong. Her body lies in the Capulet burial vault. Her soul resides with the angels. I saw her placed in the family vault and immediately rode to Mantua to tell you. Forgive me for bringing sad news, but that is my job, sir.

ROMEO   Can it be true? I defy my destiny! You know the room I am renting. Fetch me paper and ink and hire horses. I will leave tonight for Verona.

BALTHASAR   I beg you, sir, don't be hasty. You are so white-faced and frenzied that I fear you may do yourself harm.

ROMEO   Hush. You are mistaken. Do what I ordered. Didn't you bring a letter from Friar Laurence?

BALTHASAR   No, my lord.

ACT V

TRANSLATION

ROMEO   No matter. Get thee gone
                    And hire those horses. I'll be with thee straight.
                    [Exit BALTHASAR]
                    Well, Juliet, I will lie with thee to-night.
                    Let's see for means. O mischief, thou art swift   35
                    To enter in the thoughts of desperate men!
                    I do remember an apothecary,
                    And hereabouts 'a dwells, which late I noted
                    In tatt'red weeds, with overwhelming brows,
                    Culling of simples. Meagre were his looks,   40
                    Sharp misery had worn him to the bones;
                    And in his needy shop a tortoise hung,
                    An alligator stuffed, and other skins
                    Of ill-shaped fishes; and about his shelves
                    A beggarly account of empty boxes,   45
                    Green earthen pots, bladders, and musty seeds,
                    Remnants of packthread, and old cakes of roses
                    Were thinly scattered, to make up a show.
                    Noting this penury, to myself I said,
                    'An if a man did need a poison now   50
                    Whose sale is present death in Mantua,
                    Here lives a caitiff wretch would sell it him.'
                    O, this same thought did but forerun my need,
                    And this same needy man must sell it me.
                    As I remember, this should be the house.   55
                    Being holiday, the beggar's shop is shut.
                    What, ho! apothecary!
                    [Enter APOTHECARY]

APOTHECARY   Who calls so loud?

ROMEO   Come hither, man. I see that thou art poor.
                    Hold, there is forty ducats. Let me have
                    A dram of poison, such soon-speeding gear   60
                    As will disperse itself through all the veins
                    That the life-weary taker may fall dead,
                    And that the trunk may be discharged of breath
                    As violently as hasty powder fired
                    Doth hurry from the fatal cannon's womb.   65

APOTHECARY   Such mortal drugs I have; but Mantua's law
                    Is death to any he that utters them.

ORIGINAL

ROMEO	It doesn't matter. Go and hire the horses. I'll follow you immediately. *[BALTHASAR goes out]* Well, Juliet, I will join you in the tomb tonight. I must prepare for the journey. Oh bad luck, you quickly consume the minds of desperate men! I recall a pharmacist nearby, a poor man who sells medicinal herbs. He looks thin and wretched. In his threadbare shop is a tortoise shell, a stuffed alligator, and odd-shaped fish skins. On his shelves is a pathetic collection of empty boxes, mossy terra cotta pots, animal bladders, and moldy seeds, scraps of thread, and pressed roses. He scattered them about to make his shop look well stocked. When I saw how poor he was, I said to myself, "If anyone wanted to buy poison, here is a wretch who will sell it, even though it is a capital crime in Mantua." I had this thought before I needed poison. This man will surely sell it to me. As I recall, this is his house. His shop is closed for the holiday. Pharmacist! Are you at home? *[Enter APOTHECARY]*
APOTHECARY	Who calls me so loudly?
ROMEO	Come here, man. I see you are poor. Here are forty gold coins. Sell me a pinch—enough to speed through the bloodstream and immediately kill a person. I want the body as lifeless as the victim of cannon fire.
APOTHECARY	I have such poison, but it is a capital crime in Mantua to sell it.

ACT V

TRANSLATION

ROMEO	Art thou so bare and full of wretchedness
	And fearest to die? Famine is in thy cheeks,
	Need and oppression starveth in thy eyes,
	Contempt and beggary hangs upon thy back:
	The world is not thy friend, nor the world's law;
	The world affords no law to make thee rich;
	Then be not poor, but break it and take this.
APOTHECARY	My poverty but not my will consents.
ROMEO	I pay thy poverty and not thy will.
APOTHECARY	Put this in any liquid thing you will
	And drink it off, and if you had the strength
	Of twenty men, it would dispatch you straight.
ROMEO	There is thy gold—worse poison to men's souls,
	Doing more murder in this loathsome world,
	Than these poor compounds that thou mayst not sell.
	I sell thee poison; thou hast sold me none.
	Farewell. Buy food and get thyself in flesh.
	Come, cordial and not poison, go with me
	To Juliet's grave; for there must I use thee.
	[Exeunt]

ROMEO — lines 68–74 (line 70 marked)
APOTHECARY — line 75
ROMEO — line 80, 85

ORIGINAL

ROMEO	Are you poor and miserable, yet afraid to die? I see hunger on your face and suffering in your starved eyes. You look like a beggar. The world and its laws do you no favors. There is no law to make you thrive. Give up poverty by breaking Mantua's law and by taking the money.
APOTHECARY	I am poor enough to want the money, but I can't agree to break the law.
ROMEO	My money pays for your need, not your willingness.
APOTHECARY	Put this poison in any liquid and drink it down. If you were as strong as twenty men, you would still die instantly.
ROMEO	Here are the forty gold coins. Money poisons people's souls more rapidly than your drug. Greed murders more people than anything you sell in your shop. I am the one selling the poisonous money; you are guiltless. Goodbye. Buy food and fatten yourself. Come, poison. You are a refreshment, not a danger. Accompany me to Juliet's tomb. There I will drink you. *[They go out]*

ACT V

TRANSLATION

ACT V, SCENE 2

Verona. Friar Laurence's cell.

[Enter FRIAR JOHN to FRIAR LAURENCE]

JOHN	Holy Franciscan friar, brother, ho! *[Enter FRIAR LAURENCE]*
LAURENCE	This same should be the voice of Friar John. Welcome from Mantua. What says Romeo? Or, if his mind be writ, give me his letter.
JOHN	Going to find a barefoot brother out, 5 One of our order, to associate me Here in this city visiting the sick, And finding him, the searchers of the town, Suspecting that we both were in a house Where the infectious pestilence did reign, 10 Sealed up the doors, and would not let us forth, So that my speed to Mantua there was stayed.
LAURENCE	Who bare my letter, then, to Romeo?
JOHN	I could not send it—here it is again— Nor get a messenger to bring it thee, 15 So fearful were they of infection.
LAURENCE	Unhappy fortune! By my brotherhood, The letter was not nice, but full of charge, Of dear import; and the neglecting it May do much danger. Friar John, go hence, 20 Get me an iron crow and bring it straight Unto my cell.
JOHN	Brother, I'll go and bring it thee. *[Exit]*
LAURENCE	Now must I to the monument alone. Within this three hours will fair Juliet wake. She will beshrew me much that Romeo 25 Hath had no notice of these accidents; But I will write again to Mantua, And keep her at my cell till Romeo come— Poor living corse, closed in a dead man's tomb! *[Exit]*

ACT V, SCENE 2

At Friar Laurence's room in Verona.

[Enter FRIAR JOHN to FRIAR LAURENCE]

JOHN Holy friar, a member of the brotherhood of St. Francis of Assisi! *[Enter FRIAR LAURENCE]*

LAURENCE I hear Friar John's voice. Welcome back from Mantua. What did Romeo say? Did he write his reply in a letter?

JOHN When I found a fellow friar in Verona to accompany me, he was visiting the sick. The authorities feared we carried a contagious disease. They isolated us and wouldn't let us leave. The quarantine kept me from completing my errand in Mantua.

LAURENCE Who took my letter to Romeo?

JOHN The disease was so dangerous that I could not send it or hire a messenger to bring it back to you.

LAURENCE What bad luck! The letter was so important that you may have caused serious danger by not delivering it. Friar John, bring a crowbar immediately to my room.

JOHN Brother Laurence, I will hurry and fetch it. *[FRIAR JOHN goes out]*

LAURENCE I must go to the burial vault alone. Juliet will wake up in three hours. She will blame me for not informing Romeo of her fake death. I will write another letter to Romeo at Mantua. I will guard Juliet in my room until Romeo arrives. Poor girl, shut in with the dead! *[He goes out]*

ACT V

TRANSLATION

ACT V, SCENE 3

The same. A churchyard; in it a monument belonging to the Capulets.

[Enter PARIS and his Page with flowers and sweet water]

PARIS	Give me thy torch, boy. Hence, and stand aloof.
	Yet put it out, for I would not be seen.
	Under yond yew trees lay thee all along,
	Holding thy ear close to the hollow ground.
	So shall no foot upon the churchyard tread 5
	(Being loose, unfirm, with digging up of graves)
	But thou shalt hear it. Whistle then to me,
	As signal that thou hearest something approach.
	Give me those flowers. Do as I bid thee, go.
PAGE	*[Aside]* I am almost afraid to stand alone 10
	Here in the churchyard; yet I will adventure. *[Retires]*
PARIS	Sweet flower, with flowers thy bridal bed I strew
	(O woe! thy canopy is dust and stones)
	Which with sweet water nightly I will dew;
	Or, wanting that, with tears distilled by moans. 15
	The obsequies that I for thee will keep
	Nightly shall be to strew thy grave and weep.
	[Whistle Page]
	The boy gives warning something doth approach.
	What cursed foot wanders this way to-night
	To cross my obsequies and true love's rite? 20
	What, with a torch? Muffle me, night, awhile. *[Retires]*
	[Enter ROMEO and BALTHASAR with a torch,
	a mattock, and a crow of iron]
ROMEO	Give me that mattock and the wrenching iron.
	Hold, take this letter. Early in the morning
	See thou deliver it to my lord and father.
	Give me the light. Upon thy life I charge thee, 25
	Whate'er thou hearest or seest, stand all aloof
	And do not interrupt me in my course.
	Why I descend into this bed of death
	Is partly to behold my lady's face,
	But chiefly to take thence from her dead finger 30
	A precious ring—a ring that I must use
	In dear employment. Therefore hence, be gone.
	But if thou, jealous, dost return to pry
	In what I farther shall intend to do,

ORIGINAL

ACT V, SCENE 3

A cemetery in Verona at the Capulet burial vault.

[PARIS enters with his servant bearing flowers and fragrant water]

PARIS	Hand me your torch, boy. Go away and remain there. Douse the light. I don't want to be observed. Hide under those yew trees and keep your ear to the ground. If anyone come this way, you will hear the approach. Whistle a warning that someone is coming. Give me the flowers. Go. Do as I instructed.
PAGE	*[To himself]* I am afraid to be alone in a cemetery, but I will obey. *[He withdraws from sight]*
PARIS	Sweet Juliet, I drop petals on your stone tomb. Every night, I will sprinkle it with fragrant water. If I have no perfume, I will water your tomb with my tears. Every night, I will perform this ritual and weep. *[The page whistles to Paris]* My servant hears someone coming this way. What intruder is coming here tonight to interrupt my mourning for Juliet? Is that a torch I see? I will hide in the dark. *[He withdraws from sight]* *[Entering are ROMEO and BALTHASAR carrying a torch, a pickaxe, and a crowbar]*
ROMEO	Hand me the pickaxe and crowbar. Take this letter. At dawn, deliver it to my father. Hand me the torch. Swear on your life that, whatever you hear or see, you will stand out of the way and not interrupt what I do. I enter this tomb to look at my wife's face and to remove from her finger a ring. I need it. Hurry away. If you intrude on my actions,

ACT V

TRANSLATION

	By heaven, I will tear thee joint by joint	35
	And strew this hungry churchyard with thy limbs.	
	The time and my intents are savage-wild,	
	More fierce and more inexorable far	
	Than empty tigers or the roaring sea.	

BALTHASAR   I will be gone, sir, and not trouble you.   40

ROMEO   So shalt thou show me friendship. Take thou that.
Live, and be prosperous; and farewell, good fellow.

BALTHASAR   *[Aside]* For all this same, I'll hide me hereabout.
His looks I fear, and his intents I doubt. *[Retires]*

ROMEO   Thou detestable maw, thou womb of death,   45
Gorged with the dearest morsel of the earth,
Thus I enforce thy rotten jaws to open,
And in despite I'll cram thee with more food.
[ROMEO opens the tomb]

PARIS   This is that banished haughty Montague
That murd'red my love's cousin—with which grief   50
It is supposed the fair creature died—
And here is come to do some villainous shame
To the dead bodies. I will apprehend him.
Stop thy unhallowed toil, vile Montague!
Can vengeance be pursued further than death?   55
Condemned villain, I do apprehend thee.
Obey, and go with me; for thou must die.

ROMEO   I must indeed; and therefore came I hither.
Good gentle youth, tempt not a desp'rate man.
Fly hence and leave me. Think upon these gone;   60
Let them affright thee. I beseech thee, youth,
Put not another sin upon my head
By urging me to fury. O, be gone!
By heaven, I love thee better than myself,
For I come hither armed against myself.   65
Stay not, be gone. Live, and hereafter say
A madman's mercy bid thee run away.

PARIS   I do defy thy conjuration
And apprehend thee for a felon here.

ROMEO   Wilt thou provoke me? Then have at thee, boy!   70
[They fight]

PAGE   O Lord, they fight! I will go call the watch.
[Exit. PARIS falls]

ORIGINAL

	by heaven, I will tear you limb from limb and scatter your parts over this cemetery. It is a savage time of night. My purpose is also fierce, like a hungry tiger or the pounding sea.
BALTHASAR	I will go, sir, and not bother you.
ROMEO	You are a friend. Take this money. Live well. Goodbye, good Balthasar.
BALTHASAR	*[To himself]* Despite what he says, I will hide nearby. I am suspicious of his crazed eyes and actions. *[Balthasar withdraws from sight]*
ROMEO	You nest of the dead. You wicked gut filled with a precious meal. I will force your jaws open and stuff you with another body. *[ROMEO opens the tomb]*
PARIS	This is Romeo, who is exiled from Verona. He murdered Juliet's cousin Tybalt. Romeo caused her death from grief. I suspect that Romeo intends to mutilate the corpses. I will stop him. Halt your sacrilege, you despicable Montague! Can you harm your enemies even after they are dead? You exiled criminal, I have you now. Follow me or die.
ROMEO	I came here to die. Gentle Paris, don't irritate a desperate man. Leave me. Think about the dead in this tomb. Let them scare you away. I beg you, Paris, don't make me angry enough to commit another sin. Leave! By God, I care more for you than I do for myself. I came here to commit suicide. Don't wait. Go. Listen to a madman who would rather you live than die.
PARIS	I ignore your warning and seize you for your crimes.
ROMEO	Are you deliberately provoking me? Then fight me, boy! *[They fight]*
PAGE	Oh lord, Romeo and Paris are fighting! I must summon the night watchman. *[The servant departs. PARIS collapses]*

ACT V

TRANSLATION

PARIS	O, I am slain! If thou be merciful,
	Open the tomb, lay me with Juliet. *[Dies]*
ROMEO	In faith, I will. Let me peruse this face.

Mercutio's kinsman, noble County Paris! 75
What said my man when my betossed soul
Did not attend him as we rode? I think
He told me Paris should have married Juliet.
Said he not so? Or did I dream it so?
Or am I mad, hearing him talk of Juliet, 80
To think it was so? O, give me thy hand,
One writ with me in sour misfortune's book!
I'll bury thee in a triumphant grave.
A grave? O, no, a lanthorn, slaught'red youth,
For here lies Juliet, and her beauty makes 85
This vault a feasting presence full of light.
Death, lie thou there, by a dead man interred.
[Lays him in the tomb]
How oft when men are at the point of death
Have they been merry! which their keepers call
A lightning before death. O, how may I 90
Call this a lightning? O my love! my wife!
Death, that hath sucked the honey of thy breath,
Hath had no power yet upon thy beauty.
Thou art not conquered. Beauty's ensign yet
Is crimson in thy lips and in thy cheeks, 95
And death's pale flag is not advanced there.
Tybalt, liest thou there in thy bloody sheet?
O, what more favor can I do to thee
Than with that hand that cut thy youth in twain
To sunder his that was thine enemy? 100
Forgive me, cousin! Ah, dear Juliet,
Why art thou yet so fair? Shall I believe
That unsubstantial Death is amorous,
And that the lean abhorred monster keeps
Thee here in dark to be his paramour? 105
For fear of that I still will stay with thee
And never from this pallet of dim night
Depart again. Here, here will I remain
With worms that are thy chambermaids. O, here
Will I set up my everlasting rest 110
And shake the yoke of inauspicious stars
From this world-wearied flesh. Eyes, look your last!
Arms, take your last embrace! and lips, O you
The doors of breath, seal with a righteous kiss
A dateless bargain to engrossing death! 115
Come, bitter conduct; come, unsavory guide!

ORIGINAL

PARIS	Oh, I am dying! If you have any mercy, open the vault and place me beside Juliet. *[PARIS dies]*
ROMEO	I will do it. Let me see your face. You are Count Paris, Mercutio's relative! What was Balthasar saying as we rode along? I wasn't listening to him. I think he said that Paris was going to marry Juliet. Isn't that right? Or did I dream it? Am I crazy, hearing Juliet's name? Oh, let me take your hand. Both you and I are unlucky! I'll bury you in a splendid vault. A grave? Oh no, it's a lantern. Juliet's beauty fills the vault with light. Paris, lie near Juliet. You are buried by a man who will soon be dead. *[Lays him in the tomb]* Often, when men are dying, they seem happy. Physicians call their joy "light spirits before death." Oh, how can I call my feelings light? Oh, my love, my wife! Death has taken your breath, but not your beauty. Death is the loser. Juliet's lips and cheeks are still rosy. Death has not turned you pale. Tybalt, are you here in your grave garment? What favor can I do for you than to kill myself. I am the person who killed you. Forgive me, Cousin Tybalt! Ah, dear Juliet, why are you so lovely? Is death your lover? Has monstrous death turned you into his mistress? Is death afraid that I will stay with you and never leave? I will never leave this vault, where worms are your maidservants. I will stay here forever and end the misfortune that dogs me. Eyes, look once more at Juliet! Arms, hold her one last time. Lips, make your bargain with death! Come, bitter poison.

TRANSLATION

	Thou desperate pilot, now at once run on	
	The dashing rocks thy seasick weary bark!	
	Here's to my love! [Drinks] O true apothecary!	
	Thy drugs are quick. Thus with a kiss I die. *[Falls]*	120
	[Enter FRIAR LAURENCE, with lanthorn, crow, and spade]	

FRIAR   Saint Francis be my speed! How oft to-night
Have my old feet stumbled at graves! Who's there?

BALTHASAR   Here's one, a friend, and one that knows you well.

FRIAR   Bliss be upon you! Tell me, good my friend,
What torch is yond that vainly lends his light   125
To grubs and eyeless skulls? As I discern,
It burneth in the Capels' monument.

BALTHASAR   It doth so, holy sir; and there's my master,
One that you love.

FRIAR   Who is it?

BALTHASAR   Romeo.

FRIAR   How long hath he been there?

BALTHASAR   Full half an hour.   130

FRIAR   Go with me to the vault.

BALTHASAR   I dare not, sir.
My master knows not but I am gone hence,
And fearfully did menace me with death
If I did stay to look on his intents.

FRIAR   Stay then; I'll go alone. Fear comes upon me.   135
O, much I fear some ill unthrifty thing.

BALTHASAR   As I did sleep under this yew tree here,
I dreamt my master and another fought,
And that my master slew him.

FRIAR   Romeo!
Alack, alack, what blood is this which stains   140
The stony entrance of this sepulchre?
What mean these masterless and gory swords
To lie discolored by this place of peace?
[Enters the tomb]
Romeo! O, pale! Who else? What, Paris too?
And steeped in blood? Ah, what an unkind hour   145
Is guilty of this lamentable chance!
The lady stirs. *[JULIET rises]*

ORIGINAL

Come, dangerous pilot! Guide my boat into the rocks! Here's a salute to Juliet. *[He drinks poison]* Oh pharmacist! You said the truth—your drug is fast-working. I die after one more kiss to Juliet. *[ROMEO collapses] [FRIAR LAURENCE enters carrying a lantern, crowbar, and shovel]*

FRIAR Saint Francis of Assisi, hurry me along! I have stumbled frequently tonight over graves. Who's there?

BALTHASAR I am a friend. You know me well.

FRIAR May you be happy! Tell me, friend, whose torch lights up earthworms and skulls? It seems to light up the Capulet vault.

BALTHASAR It does, holy friar. There's my master, whom you love.

FRIAR Who is it?

BALTHASAR Romeo.

FRIAR How long has he been there?

BALTHASAR A half hour.

FRIAR Go with me to the vault.

BALTHASAR I can't, sir. Romeo thinks I have gone away. He promised to kill me if I stayed and watched what he did.

FRIAR Stay here, then. I will go alone. I am afraid. I fear some terrible sight.

BALTHASAR While I slept under that yew tree, I dreamed that Romeo fought another man and killed him.

FRIAR Romeo! Whose blood splashed the door of this stone tomb? Whose weapons are these lying blood-drenched in this peaceful place? *[Enters the tomb]* Romeo! How pale you are! And who is this? Paris, you too? And covered with blood. This is the scene of a terrible fight. Juliet is waking up. *[JULIET sits up]*

ACT V

TRANSLATION

JULIET	O comfortable friar! Where is my lord?
	I do remember well where I should be,
	And there I am. Where is my Romeo? 150
FRIAR	I hear some noise. Lady, come from that nest
	Of death, contagion, and unnatural sleep.
	A greater power than we can contradict
	Hath thwarted our intents. Come, come away.
	Thy husband in thy bosom there lies dead; 155
	And Paris too. Come, I'll dispose of thee
	Among a sisterhood of holy nuns.
	Stay not to question, for the watch is coming.
	Come, go, good Juliet. I dare no longer stay.
JULIET	Go, get thee hence, for I will not away. 160
	[Exit FRIAR]
	What's here? A cup, closed in my true love's hand?
	Poison, I see, hath been his timeless end.
	O churl! drunk all, and left no friendly drop
	To help me after? I will kiss thy lips.
	Haply some poison yet doth hang on them 165
	To make me die with a restorative. *[Kisses him]*
	Thy lips are warm!
CHIEF WATCHMAN	*[Within]* Lead, boy. Which way?
JULIET	Yea, noise? Then I'll be brief. O happy dagger!
	[Snatches Romeo's dagger]
	This is thy sheath; there rust, and let me die. 170
	[She stabs herself and falls. Enter Paris's Page and Watch]
PAGE	This is the place. There, where the torch doth burn.
CHIEF WATCHMAN	The ground is bloody. Search about the churchyard.
	Go, some of you; whoe'er you find attach.
	[Exeunt some of the Watch]
	Pitiful sight! Here lies the County slain;
	And Juliet bleeding, warm, and newly dead, 175
	Who here hath lain this two days buried.
	Go, tell the Prince; run to the Capulets;
	Raise up the Montagues; some others search.
	[Exeunt others of the Watch]
	We see the ground whereon these woes do lie,
	But the true ground of all these piteous woes 180
	We cannot without circumstance descry.
	[Enter some of the Watch, with Romeo's Man BALTHASAR]

ORIGINAL

JULIET	Oh comforting friar! Where is Romeo? I remember where I am. Where is Romeo?
FRIAR	I hear a noise. Juliet, come from this infectious cemetery and your long sleep. Fate has ruined our plans. Come with me. Here are Romeo and Paris. Both are dead. Come with me. I will find a place for you at a convent. Don't try to understand. The night watchman is coming. Come with me, Juliet. I can't stay here any longer.
JULIET	Go without me. I won't leave. *[FRIAR LAURENCE leaves]* What is this—a cup of poison in Romeo's hand? I see that poison killed him. Oh, villain. You drank all of it and left me none. I will kiss the poison on your lips. Perhaps a drop of poison will help me die with you. *[She kisses ROMEO]* Your lips are still warm!
CHIEF WATCHMAN	*[Offstage]* Lead me, boy. Which way are you taking me?
JULIET	A noise? Then I must act quickly. Oh handy dagger! *[She grabs ROMEO'S dagger]* My breast is your sheath. There rust and let me die. *[She stabs herself and collapses. PARIS'S servant and the night watchman enter]*
PAGE	This is the place. Over there where you see the burning torch.
CHIEF WATCHMAN	There is blood on the ground. Search the cemetery. Arrest anyone you find. *[Some night watchmen depart]* What a pity! Here is the corpse of Count Paris. Juliet is dead, but warm and bleeding. She has been buried for two days. Go tell Prince Escalus. Run to the Capulet house. Call the Montagues. Some others search the cemetery. *[Other night watchmen depart]* Look at the ground. I can see the outcome of the fight, but I can't determine the causes. *[A night watchman enters with ROMEO'S servant BALTHASAR]*

ACT V

TRANSLATION

SECOND WATCHMAN	Here's Romeo's man. We found him in the churchyard.
CHIEF WATCHMAN	Hold him in safety till the Prince come hither. *[Enter FRIAR LAURENCE and another Watchman]*
THIRD WATCHMAN	Here is a friar that trembles, sighs, and weeps. We took this mattock and this spade from him 185 As he was coming from this churchyard side.
CHIEF WATCHMAN	A great suspicion. Stay the friar too. *[Enter the PRINCE and Attendants]*
PRINCE	What misadventure is so early up, That calls our person from our morning rest? *[Enter CAPULET and his WIFE with others]*
CAPULET	What should it be, that is so shrieked abroad? 190
WIFE	O the people in the street cry 'Romeo,' Some 'Juliet,' and some 'Paris'; and all run, With open outcry, toward our monument.
PRINCE	What fear is this which startles in your ears?
CHIEF WATCHMAN	Sovereign, here lies the County Paris slain; 195 And Romeo dead; and Juliet, dead before, Warm and new killed.
PRINCE	Search, seek, and know how this foul murder comes.
CHIEF WATCHMAN	Here is a friar, and slaughtered Romeo's man, With instruments upon them fit to open 200 These dead men's tombs.
CAPULET	O heavens! O wife, look how our daughter bleeds! This dagger hath mista'en, for, lo, his house Is empty on the back of Montague, And it missheathed in my daughter's bosom! 205
WIFE	O me! this sight of death is as a bell That warns my old age to a sepulchre. *[Enter MONTAGUE and others]*
PRINCE	Come Montague; for thou art early up To see thy son and heir more early down.
MONTAGUE	Alas, my liege, my wife is dead to-night! 210 Grief of my son's exile hath stopped her breath. What further woe conspires against mine age?
PRINCE	Look, and thou shalt see.

ORIGINAL

SECOND WATCHMAN	Here is Balthasar, Romeo's servant. We found him in the cemetery.
CHIEF WATCHMAN	Hold him until Prince Escalus arrives. *[FRIAR LAURENCE and another watchman arrive]*
THIRD WATCHMAN	We found Friar Laurence, who is trembling, sorrowing, and crying. We took his pickaxe and shovel as he was leaving the cemetery.
CHIEF WATCHMAN	Very suspicious. Hold the friar as well as Balthasar. *[PRINCE ESCALUS and his servants enter]*
PRINCE	What crime requires me to leave my bed so early in the morning? *[CAPULET and his WIFE enter with other people]*
CAPULET	What is causing all these cries in the city?
WIFE	People in the street call the names of Romeo, Juliet, and Paris. Citizens are shrieking and hurrying toward our family vault.
PRINCE	What is the cause of all this clamor?
CHIEF WATCHMAN	Prince, here lies Count Paris. He has been murdered. Romeo is dead and Juliet, who died two days ago, is newly killed and her body still warm.
PRINCE	Investigate the cause of these killings.
CHIEF WATCHMAN	Here are Friar Laurence and Balthasar, Romeo's servant. They carry tools for breaking into tombs.
CAPULET	Oh heavens! Wife, look at the blood from Juliet's body! This dagger from Romeo's sheath has pierced Juliet's chest!
WIFE	Oh me! These deaths may kill me. *[MONTAGUE and others enter]*
PRINCE	Montague, it is early in the morning for you to see your son Romeo newly killed.
MONTAGUE	Alas, Prince, my wife died tonight! She died mourning Romeo's banishment. What other tragedy threatens an old man?
PRINCE	Look and see for yourself.

ACT V

TRANSLATION

MONTAGUE	O thou untaught! What manners is in this,
	To press before thy father to a grave? 215

PRINCE	Seal up the mouth of outrage for a while,
	Till we can clear these ambiguities
	And know their spring, their head, their true descent;
	And then will I be general of your woes
	And lead you even to death. Meantime forbear, 220
	And let mischance be slave to patience.
	Bring forth the parties of suspicion.

FRIAR	I am the greatest, able to do least,
	Yet most suspected, as the time and place
	Doth make against me, of this direful murder; 225
	And here I stand, both to impeach and purge
	Myself condemned and myself excused.

PRINCE	Then say at once what thou dost know in this.

FRIAR	I will be brief, for my short date of breath
	Is not so long as is a tedious tale. 230
	Romeo, there dead, was husband to that Juliet;
	And she, there dead, that Romeo's faithful wife.
	I married them; and their stol'n marriage day
	Was Tybalt's doomsday, whose untimely death
	Banished the new-made bridegroom from this city; 235
	For whom, and not for Tybalt, Juliet pined.
	You, to remove that siege of grief from her,
	Betrothed and would have married her perforce
	To County Paris. Then comes she to me
	And with wild looks bid me devise some mean 240
	To rid her from this second marriage,
	Or in my cell there would she kill herself.
	Then gave I her (so tutored by my art)
	A sleeping potion; which so took effect
	As I intended, for it wrought on her 245
	The form of death. Meantime I writ to Romeo
	That he should hither come as this dire night
	To help to take her from her borrowed grave,
	Being the time the potion's force should cease.
	But he which bore my letter, Friar John, 250
	Was stayed by accident, and yesternight
	Returned my letter back. Then all alone
	At the prefixed hour of her waking
	Came I to take her from her kindred's vault;
	Meaning to keep her closely at my cell 255
	Till I conveniently could send to Romeo.
	But when I came, some minute ere the time
	Of her awakening, here untimely lay

ORIGINAL

MONTAGUE	Oh son! Why have you died so young?
PRINCE	Stop your mourning. I must first investigate these crimes. Then I will answer your questions and condemn to death the guilty party. Meanwhile, be patient. Bring the suspects to me.
FRIAR	I look guilty for being here at the time of these killings. I am ready to tell you what I know.
PRINCE	Tell me at once.
FRIAR	I will be brief. Romeo was Juliet's husband. Juliet was Romeo's wife. I performed their wedding ceremony on the same day that Tybalt died. Because of Tybalt's murder, Romeo was exiled from Verona. Juliet mourned for Romeo, not for Tybalt. The Capulets tried to relieve her grief by betrothing her to Count Paris. Frenzied by her dilemma, she came to my room the day after her wedding and threatened to kill herself if I didn't intervene. I gave her a drug that made her appear dead. I wrote a letter to Romeo in Mantua asking him to meet me at the Capulet burial vault before Juliet woke up. Unfortunately, Friar John could not deliver the letter and returned it to me. I came to remove her from the family vault. I intended to keep her at my room until I could send for Romeo.

ACT V

The noble Paris and true Romeo dead.
She wakes; and I entreated her come forth   260
And bear this work of heaven with patience;
But then a noise did scare me from the tomb,
And she, too desperate, would not go with me,
But, as it seems, did violence on herself.
All this I know, and to the marriage   265
Her nurse is privy; and if aught in this
Miscarried by my fault, let my old life
Be sacrificed, some hour before his time,
Unto the rigor of severest law.

PRINCE   We still have known thee for a holy man.   270
Where's Romeo's man? What can he say in this?

BALTHASAR   I brought my master news of Juliet's death;
And then in post he came from Mantua
To this same place, to this same monument.
This letter he early bid me give his father,   275
And threat'ned me with death, going in the vault,
If I departed not and left him there.

PRINCE   Give me the letter. I will look on it.
Where is the County's page that raised the watch?
Sirrah, what made your master in this place?   280

PAGE   He came with flowers to strew his lady's grave;
And bid me stand aloof, and so I did.
Anon comes one with light to ope the tomb;
And by and by my master drew on him;
And then I ran away to call the watch.   285

PRINCE   This letter doth make good the friar's words,
Their course of love, the tidings of her death;
And here he writes that he did buy a poison
Of a poor pothecary, and therewithal
Came to this vault to die, and lie with Juliet.   290
Where be these enemies? Capulet, Montague,
See what a scourge is laid upon your hate,
That heaven finds means to kill your joys with love.
And I, for winking at your discords too,
Have lost a brace of kinsmen. All are punished.   295

CAPULET   O brother Montague, give me thy hand
This is my daughter's jointure, for no more
Can I demand.

When I arrived before her waking, I found Paris and
Romeo both dead. Juliet began stirring. I begged her to
leave the tomb and bear the grief of Romeo's death.
A noise frightened me away from the vault. Juliet, in the
depths of grief, would not leave. Instead, she appears to
have killed herself. That is all I know. Juliet's nurse was
aware of the secret marriage. If these deaths are my
fault, kill me according to the law.

PRINCE	You have always been a holy man. Where is Balthasar? What can he add to this testimony?
BALTHASAR	I reported Juliet's death to Romeo. He left Mantua and arrived at this tomb. He left a letter for his father. Romeo threatened to kill me if I didn't leave him in the vault.
PRINCE	Give me the letter. I want to read it. Where is the servant of Count Paris, who called the night watchman? Sir, what was Paris doing here in the cemetery?
PAGE	He brought flowers to sprinkle on Juliet's tomb. He told me to stay away from this place. I did as I was told. I saw someone carry a torch here. Paris drew his sword against the man. I ran to get the night watchman.
PRINCE	This letter corroborates Friar Laurence's testimony. It tells of Romeo's love for Juliet and the news of her death. Romeo explains that he bought poison from a pharmacist in Mantua. Romeo came to this tomb to die next to Juliet. Where are the feuding families? Capulet and Montague, see what tragedy has grown from your hatred. God has killed your children, who were in love. For allowing this feud to continue, I have lost two relatives, Mercutio and Paris. All are punished.
CAPULET	Montague, my brother, take my hand. This is my daughter's reward. I can't ask anything else.

ACT V

TRANSLATION

MONTAGUE   But I can give thee more;
                    For I will raise her statue in pure gold,
                    That whiles Verona by that name is known,   300
                    There shall no figure at such rate be set
                    As that of true and faithful Juliet.

CAPULET   As rich shall Romeo's by his lady lie—
                    Poor sacrifices of our enmity!

PRINCE   A glooming peace this morning with it brings   305
                    The sun for sorrow will not show his head.
                    Go hence, to have more talk of these sad things;
                    Some shall be pardoned, and some punished;
                    For never was a story of more woe
                    Than this of Juliet and her Romeo. *[Exeunt]*   310

ORIGINAL

MONTAGUE	I pledge something more. I will commission a gold statue of Juliet. So long as Verona exists, no one will be so valued as faithful Juliet.
CAPULET	I will honor Romeo, who lies by his wife—what a waste of lives over our feud!
PRINCE	This site is so gloomy that the sun will not rise. Go and discuss this tragedy. I will pardon some people and punish others. There never was a sadder story than that of the lovers Juliet and Romeo. *[They go out]*

ACT V

TRANSLATION

Questions for Reflection

1. How would you describe the horrors of the final scene, which takes place in a dimly lighted cemetery? Why do multiple deaths derive from the feud between the Capulets and Montagues? How much of the tragedy is the fault of Friar Laurence? of Friar John? of Lady Capulet? of Capulet? of Prince Escalus?

2. How does the death of Tybalt compare with that of Paris? Consider Romeo's hesitance to fight the two men. In Act V, why does Romeo still feel guilty about Tybalt's death? Why does Romeo consider Paris a friend?

3. Which lines from the play indicate multiple family relationships that include Tybalt, Mercutio, Montague, Capulet, Prince Escalus, Lady Capulet, Lady Montague, Romeo, and Juliet? What other relationships does Capulet's invitation to his guests describe? Explain how faulty community relations dominate the action. Why do Capulet and his wife both refer to Tybalt's father as "my brother"?

4. How do Friar Laurence, the nurse, the Capulets, and the Montagues contrast as advisers to Romeo and Juliet? How does Susan's death contribute to the nurse's love for Juliet?

5. How would you describe Romeo's romance with Rosaline? Contrast her response to his courtship with Juliet's introduction to Romeo. Why is Friar Laurence dubious about Romeo's sincerity toward his love for the two girls? Why do Romeo's friends taunt him for his extreme lovesickness?

6. How does Prince Escalus gather evidence at the scene of multiple crimes, including the stabbing death of a woman already assumed to be dead? What do Friar Laurence and Balthasar contribute to the investigation? Why is Romeo's letter important?

7. What are the responses to Romeo's love for Juliet? Consider the words of Friar Laurence, the nurse, Capulet, Montague, Benvolio, Juliet, Balthasar, and Mercutio.

8. How does Shakespeare present the causes and symptoms of romance? What does Romeo observe while he hides in the Capulet orchard? Why does the nurse urge Juliet to forget the marriage and accept Paris as a more appropriate suitor?

9. Why is Mercutio's death a turning point in the tragedy? Account for the popularity of his lyric speeches with famous actors. How might William Shakespeare have honored Christopher Marlowe by portraying his violent bar-room death through the death of Mercutio in a street brawl?

10. How would you compose an extended definition of character flaw as it applies to Romeo? Consider evidence of his immaturity, vengeance, rash extremes, and self-absorbed dramatizing. Why does Romeo still appeal to audiences? to Lady Montague? to Juliet? to Friar Laurence? to Balthasar? to the Veronese?

11. How do the situations in Verona at the beginning and end of the play compare? Why do the two young lovers appear to be martyrs to civil peace and to forgiveness?

12. How would you account for Friar John's failure to deliver the letter to Romeo in Mantua? Why was quarantine necessary during the Renaissance? Why do Franciscan friars appear admirable for their devotion to the sick?

13. Why does Shakespeare depict Friar Laurence as a skilled herbalist, a devout Franciscan friar, a brother to other Franciscans, a supporter of civil peace, a loving confessor, a wise marriage counselor, a coward, a meddler, and a bumbling fool?

14. What do you think the effect of the gold statue on the citizens of Verona, including relatives of both the Capulets and the Montagues, will be? What other remnants of the brief marriage of Romeo and Juliet survive at the end of the play?

15. What is the importance of above-the-ground burial to the action? Why does Friar Laurence fear that Juliet is in danger of awakening in an atmosphere of contagion and horror? How does she prove him wrong? How does Shakespeare create irony from Friar Laurence's fears? What other characters fear graveyards at night?

16. What are the differences in the rearing of boys and girls in Verona as evidenced in the play? Consider Romeo's pacing the outdoors at dawn, Juliet's chaperonage, Romeo's freedom from parental control,

Juliet's immurement in her room after the feast, Romeo's retreat to Friar Laurence's cell, Friar Laurence's proposal to send Juliet to a convent, Romeo's friendship with armed companions, and Juliet's need of permission to go to confession. Why does gendered courtship condemn Juliet to marry a second time? Why does Capulet believe that Juliet will agree to the arranged marriage with Paris? How does a father's anger contribute to the tragedy?

17. How does Shakespeare contrast light and dark throughout the play? Why does Romeo visit the orchard in the dark? Why does Juliet declare that the birdsong is that of a nightingale rather than a lark? Why does Romeo consider her a "bright angel"? How does Romeo perpetuate the notion of brightness when he views Juliet in the tomb? How do torches conclude the play?

18. How would you explain the theme of fate as it applies to Romeo and Juliet? Why are unlucky lovers "star-crossed"? How does fate alter the proposed wedding from Thursday to Wednesday, hinder Friar John, speed Balthasar from Verona to Mantua, introduce Romeo to the source of poison, bring about Paris's death near his wife-to-be, spoil Friar Laurence's plan to save Juliet from a second marriage, cause Lady Montague's death, and end the feud between the Capulets and Montagues?

19. What accounts for the reading of a letter from Romeo to his father so soon after Romeo's death? How does Shakespeare spare Romeo's mother a worse grief than her son's exile to Mantua?

20. How would you compose an extended definition of courtship ritual based on the relationship between Paris and Juliet? Why do two males—a father and a potential groom—discuss Juliet without asking her opinion of the arrangement? How do they misjudge her grief for Tybalt's death? Why do Lady Capulet and the nurse pressure Juliet to marry Paris?

21. What is the relationship between Tybalt and Capulet? What does Capulet observe about Tybalt's temper at the feast? Why is Tybalt known as the "prince of cats"? Why does no one charge Tybalt with a hot temper after his death?

22. How would the play be changed if Romeo had taken Juliet with him into exile in Mantua? What factors could have turned their elopement into tragedy?

23. How would you define Gothic convention using examples from the graveyard scene and from the seeming death of Juliet from the herb that Friar Laurence recommends? Consider how a torch-lit vault, yew trees, crowbars, an empty vial, cries of night watchmen, a twice-dead corpse, bloody ground, a murder investigation, and Tybalt's shroud contribute to Shakespeare's Gothicism. Why are hand-to-hand fighting and two suicides at the Capulet vault a favorite scene for actors and audiences?

24. Why does Shakespeare depict Lady Capulet and the nurse as weaker and less influential than male characters? What actions make Juliet seem easily led? Why does she give up her family in favor of marriage to Romeo? How does Juliet emerge as a strong-minded wife in the final scene?

25. How does Shakespeare reveal that Prince Escalus suffers for his great-heartness and lenience? Why does Tybalt deserve to die in the street? How does the sentence of banishment suit Romeo's crime?

26. How do astral and planetary images advance the theme of ill luck in the play? Why is it better to swear by the sun than by the moon? Why are Juliet's eyes a replacement for the stars?

27. What does Shakespeare imply about the cause and spread of family feuds? Why does the play emphasize Capulet's advancing age? What details suggest that Lady Capulet is still in her twenties?

28. How does the last scene typify human failing? What aspects of the peace-making between families suggest that a gold statue will not make up for the loss of so many young citizens?

29. What details are essential to a staging of the play? Rank in terms of importance these elements: bird calls, an earthquake, Juliet's ring, the rope ladder, torches, swords, pickaxe and shovel, poison, betrothal, Rosaline, an orchard, 40 ducats, Lammastide, lanterns, a shroud, an empty vial, an undelivered letter, a quarantine, deadly herbs, masking, the Franciscan brotherhood, and an invitation to a feast.

30. How does Shakespeare please both groundlings and more discerning playgoers with *Romeo and Juliet*? What aspects of the play would please both extremes of drama appreciation? What themes are universal? poignant? unsettling? life-affirming?

31. How does Shakespeare justify the downfall of so young a couple as Romeo and Juliet? Why does the play stress the need for sacrifice to end a family feud?

32. What roles do Gregory, Sampson, a pharmacist, Rosaline, Susan, the page, Balthasar, the nurse's husband, Abram, sick Mantuans, musicians, party guests, outraged citizens, the nightwatch, cooks, and Friar John play in the tragedy? Why does Shakespeare present some episodes through narrative rather than action—for example, Rosaline's refusal of Romeo, Susan's death, an earthquake, Lady Montague's death, and the day that Juliet fell and injured her forehead?

33. What aspects of Romeo's character appeal to stage and film actors? Which speeches reveal nobility, wit, idealism, rashness, vulnerability, friendship, regret, and immaturity?

34. Is Paris justified in insisting that Romeo is guilty of the deaths of Tybalt and Juliet? Why does Paris suspect Romeo of grave robbing and corpse mutilation? What punishment does Paris demand for disturbing a burial vault?

35. How do Mercutio and Romeo complement each other's strengths and weaknesses? Why does their friendship thrive? Why does the play depict Mercutio as imaginative and witty? How does his death precipitate mulitple losses?

36. What does Prince Escalus discover during his investigation? Does he have grounds to charge Friar Laurence with a crime? Does Friar Laurence abide by the rules of the Franciscan brotherhood?

37. What role does literacy play in *Romeo and Juliet*? How does the issue of literacy affect the plot?

38. How does Shakespeare honor young love? Why does a hasty marriage derserve validation? How might grandchildren have eased family enmity?

39. Why does the play stress the fragility of life? How do the deaths of the Capulet's other children, Susan, Tybalt, Paris, Romeo, Mercutio, and Juliet make youth seem more precious?

40. Why does Shakespeare stress suicidal thoughts? When do Romeo and Juliet each ponder suicide? What does a double suicide indicate about their love? their despair? their relationship with adults?

Notes

Notes

Notes

Notes

Notes

Notes

Notes

Notes

Notes